THE HOUSEWIFE ASSASSIN'S DEADLY DOSSIER

JOSIE BROWN

A BOOK BY

SIGNAL
PRESS

Library of Congress Cataloging-in-Publication Data is available upon request

Cover Design by Andrew Brown, ClickTwiceDesign.com

Digital Formatting by Austin Brown, CheapEbookFormatting.com

Trade Paperback ISBN: 978-1-942052-17-3

Hardcover ISBN: 978-1-942052-31-9

V022319

"This is a super sexy and fun read that you shouldn't miss! A kick ass woman that can literally kick ass as well as cook and clean. Donna gives a whole new meaning to "taking out the trash."
—Mary Jacobs, *Book Hounds Reviews*

"*The Housewife Assassin's Handbook* by Josie Brown is a fun, sexy and intriguing mystery. Donna Stone is a great heroine —housewives can lead all sorts of double lives, but as an assassin? Who would have seen that one coming? It's a fast-paced read, the gadgets are awesome, and I could just picture Donna fighting off Russian gangsters and skinheads all the while having a pie at home cooling on the windowsill. As a housewife myself, this book was a fantastic escape that had me dreaming "if only" the whole way through. The book doesn't take itself too seriously, which makes for the perfect combination of mystery and humour."
—*Curled Up with a Good Book and a Cup of Tea*

"*The Housewife Assassin's Handbook* is a hilarious, laugh-out-loud read. Donna is a fantastic character–practical, witty, and kick-ass tough. There's plenty of action–both in and out of the bedroom… I especially love the housekeeping tips at the start of each chapter–each with its own deadly twist! This book is perfect for relaxing in the bath with after a long day. I can't wait to read the next in the series. Highly Recommended!"

—*CrimeThrillerGirl.com*

"This was an addictive read–gritty but funny at the same time. I ended up reading it in just one evening and couldn't go to sleep until I knew what the outcome would be! It was action-packed and humorous from the start, and that continued throughout, I was pleased to discover that this is the first of a series and look forward to getting my hands on Book Two so I can see where life takes Donna and her family next!"

—*Me, My Books, and I*

"The two halves of Donna's life make sense. As you follow her story, there's no point where you think of her as "Assassin Donna" vs. "Mummy Donna', her attitude to life is even throughout. I really like how well this is done. And as for Jack. I'll have one of those, please?"

—*The Northern Witch's Book Blog*

Novels in The Housewife Assassin Series

A Hard Man is Good to Find

In espionage parlance, a "hard man" is an assassin: someone whose profession is to kill those stealing others' secrets or spouting inconvenient truths.

Should one appear on your doorstep with a mission to exterminate, any attempt to outrun your caller will earn you a bullet in the back.

Think you'll stave off the inevitable with an offer of "Coffee, tea, or me?" He may take you up on all three, but the bottom line is that his mission comes first.

Then again, so does your lust—for life.

Instead, invite him in and offer him a cuppa joe, along with something that will even the playing field:

A sprinkle of lye, as opposed to creamer, followed by going off the grid for good.

~

CARL STONE ALMOST MISSED HIS FLIGHT OUT OF VANCOUVER because his target refused to die.

It should have been an easy hit. The target, a portly Canadian defense contractor with a heart condition, was selling his country's missile launch codes—not only to an international terrorist group, but to the Chinese as well.

A traitor was one thing. A traitor who double-dipped on what was supposed to be exclusive intel was an accident waiting to happen.

Fat Ass's life insurance policy was about to be cancelled.

The man's medical charts showed that his enlarged prostate sent him to the john at least twice an hour. And since he was a stickler for getting to his departure gate at least an hour before wheels-up, all Carl had to do was wait until Fat Ass was hit with the urge to take one more bathroom break. After the extermination, Carl would hop his own flight home to Los Angeles, which was scheduled out of YVR around the same time as Fat Ass's flight.

He didn't have to wait long. Five minutes after Fat Ass checked in with the gate attendant, he went in search of the nearest men's room.

Carl was a step ahead of him. He was dressed in a janitor's uniform, so no one questioned him as he rolled a mop and bucket in front of the door and placed an OUT OF ORDER sign on the handle. After he rousted the two guys zipping up in front of the urinal, he went back outside so that he could greet Fat Ass with the assurance that "the floor should be dry by now, so go on in."

Fat Ass barely acknowledged him with a nod, let alone a thank you.

Carl left the sign on the doorknob and followed Fat Ass

into the restroom with the mop and rolling bucket, locking the door behind them.

Fat Ass was mid-whiz when Carl pricked him in the back of his thigh with the needle filled with succinylcholine—probably not the best time to do so, because Fat Ass's response was to turn around, dick in hand.

"What the hell!" they shouted in unison—Carl because Fat Ass sprayed his very expensive John Lobb brogues with urine, and Fat Ass because, let's face it, that needle hurt like hell.

Fat Ass was shocked, but Carl was angry. The shoes were a thou a pair! Still, he resisted the urge to punch the guy in the throat, which would cause him to double over, at which point Carl would bash his head against the wall and toss him onto the tile floor to stomp to a bloody pulp—

But only because that would defeat the purpose of making the hit look like an accidental death, as per his client's instructions.

By now, Fat Ass was onto the fact that Carl was there to kill him. Having no lethal weapon, but fully aware that Carl was concerned about the condition of his shoes, he brandished his spraying organ in his assailant's direction.

In the best of all possible worlds, by now the guy would have fallen backward into Carl's arms so that he could drag him into one of the stalls and heave him up on a toilet for some harried traveler to find. An autopsy would reveal he'd had a heart attack when he sat down for a grunt.

"Die already, you son of a bitch," Carl hissed at the man as he dodged the spray as best as he could. If his fancy footwork couldn't save his shoes, maybe it would wear out Fat

Ass, who seemed to have the constitution—not to mention the pissing power—of a rhino.

Carl's light-footedness seemed to do the trick. Fat Ass's chest must have started tightening up on him because one hand dropped limply to his side.

Finally, thought Carl.

Noting that the Canadian was leaning back, he positioned himself to catch the slumping hulk—

Only to have to leap in front of the man in time to cradle him before he fell to his knees or cracked his head on the tile.

Metaphorically speaking, with death comes relief. But in this case, Fat Ass also relieved what was left in his bladder all over Carl's shoes.

"Damn it," Carl swore again.

His damp shoes squeaked as he hauled the body into the nearest stall and shoved it up onto the john. By bending Fat Ass's knees and positioning them far enough apart, the body might just resist the gravitational pull to fall to the floor long enough for Carl's plane to be wheels up.

He had just mopped up the puddles of piss when he heard the sob. He froze. Was it coming from Fat Ass's stall? How the hell could that be?

He stayed perfectly still. Minutes went by that seemed like hours.

A flushing sound came from one of the next stalls.

Shit, Carl thought. He slowly removed the knife concealed in his trouser leg and flicked it open. His steps toward the stall were slow and silent.

The door creaked open.

Out popped a head.

It belonged to a boy. He couldn't be any more than nine years old.

Still, the boy had heard everything. Maybe he'd even seen what happened through the crack between the door and the stall.

Having a witness to one of his hits was a first for Carl.

The boy shook while Carl thought through his options. In this case, a knife wasn't necessary. He could pinch the boy's nostrils and suffocate him in less than two minutes. But if he killed the kid, it would be too much of a coincidence that two people had died in the same restroom on the same day.

I'm no monster, Carl told himself.

For the first time since he'd become a hard man, he had a chance to prove it.

No one had jiggled the restroom door's lock, so the sign was certainly keeping everyone away. But surely the kid's parents were looking for him by now and beginning to panic as well. Carl knew he'd be freaking out if it were one of his children. He had two kids of his own: his daughter, Mary, was seven. His son, Jeff, would be five tomorrow. This was one of the reasons he had to make it home tonight.

He wondered what Jeff would do in the same situation.

Just at that moment, the boy raised his head. His eyes sought out Carl's. Then the boy reached out to him. He held something in his hand—a Wolverine action figure. "You... can have it, if you want."

Carl stared down at it. Finally he muttered, "Thanks." He kneeled down so that he was eye level with the boy. "What did you see?"

The boy blinked once and pursed his lips. "Not...nothing," he whispered.

"It's time to go."

The boy nodded. Carl guided him to the door, opened it and followed him out.

The boy ran off to the left. Carl bent down and pretended to tie his shoe, but he watched as a woman, perhaps three gates down, shouted at the boy. He turned. Finding her, he ran into her arms. The look in her eyes went from frenzy to relief. Whatever he said to her had her looking back toward the restroom.

By then, Carl was buried deep in the throng of travelers crisscrossing the terminal.

A moment later, he was in the janitor's closet, where he changed back into his business suit.

Carl's Air Canada flight to LA was out of YVR's international terminal. On the way, he passed several Canadian Air Transportation Security guards. To make his flight, he knew he'd have to make a run for it. Instead, he forced himself to walk as if he didn't have a care in the world.

When he got to his departure gate, an Air Canada agent was already in the process of locking the door to the jetway. Carl practically threw his boarding pass at the woman as he ran past her.

Once in his seat, he pulled out a cell phone and texted his client contact, EW, the signal that the extermination went off without a hitch:

Have a nice day!

But because this wasn't exactly true, Carl sent a second text, this one to his employer, the black-ops organization known as Acme Industries. It read:

Clean-up on Aisle Five

No doubt the airport's security cameras would validate

the young boy's tall tale of a janitor assassin. Carl's boss, Ryan Clancy, would have to alert the Canadian Security and Intelligence Service about the hiccup in the mission.

The last thing either Carl or Ryan would want is for the client—an organization known as the Quorum—to know something had gone wrong. Otherwise, the Quorum would never trust Carl again. After all, he had been hired as a freelancer.

He'd done so in order to infiltrate the organization, at the behest of Acme's first and foremost client, the Central Intelligence Agency.

Noting the evil eye from the flight attendant who had already given him a hard time for holding up the plane, he snapped off his phone.

He slept on the three-hour flight home. Those he exterminated never haunted his dreams.

But this time, he dreamt of the little boy.

As always, Carl's wife, Donna, was waiting curbside at LAX's passenger arrival door. His children, Mary and Jeff, ran up to their father. As they smothered him with kisses, he lifted one child in each arm and hugged them to his chest.

When they finally let him go, he reached down into his valise and pulled out the Wolverine doll. "A birthday present," he said, as he handed it to Jeff.

The little boy held it up, then ran with it back to the car, where his mother was waiting.

"What did you get me?" Mary asked her father as she curled her hand in his.

He held up her hand and kissed it. "I came home, safe and sound."

"But you always do that, Daddy," she said with a pout.

"And I always will," he promised.

It never once bothered Carl Stone that he led a double life. In fact, he took pride in the ease in which he brushed off the cold emotionless demeanor that came with his job as a paid killer.

The same meticulous planning that went into his kills had been used in wooing his wife, Donna, whom he loved unconditionally. She was the rock on which his ideals were based. She was the beacon of light that guided him through the dark and treacherous undercurrents of his chosen profession, where money talked and power ruled supreme. Despite having neither, Carl vowed to, one day, reign supreme. His plotting and scheming skills would assure this, too.

The warm, welcoming smile that had Mary and Jeff leaping into his arms also lured his targets closer to him without ever realizing their lives were in danger.

And the index finger that slowly but firmly pulled the trigger on his M40 was the same one he used to bring his wife to ecstatic climax during foreplay—although arguably at a more frenetic and sustained pace all the way through the lovemaking that followed.

The kids had fallen asleep on the trip back from the airport. He'd picked up Mary, who was the heavier of the two, while Donna hugged Jeff to her chest and followed him into the house.

It took Donna and Carl just a few minutes to tuck the children into their tiny bunk beds.

It took a few seconds for them to strip out of their clothes and fall into the king-sized bed they shared.

He took her in his arms as if he'd never let her go. Eventually, his hands would roam over her body, his fingertips lightly skimming every curve—her plump breasts, her rounded hips, then onto the soft valley of her belly—before gently probing the sweet spot between her thighs.

In turn, her kisses revived him.

He never failed to feel a charge of anticipation when her lips roamed down onto his chest, or when her tongue circled his nipples, before moving down the taut ribbed plane of his abdomen.

Her touch never failed to harden him.

When finally he was inside of her—when he could feel her heart pounding practically in his chest, when he felt her hot breath rise in his nostrils—he felt they were one body.

As was always the case, it was after making love to Donna that he felt closest to her. During this precious moment between them, he wondered if she could read his thoughts, too. Why else would she give that deep, shy laugh that always made his heart skip a beat, and whisper into his hear in a singsong sort of way, "I know what you're thinking…"

No, you don't, he was tempted to say. *But boy, wouldn't it be interesting if you did?*

He wondered how she'd react to the news that he'd murdered Fat Ass just a few hours ago. Or that just last week, when he was supposed to be in Chicago, he stalked a woman through the Bolivian jungle, taking her down with an eight-hundred-foot shot to the back of her head.

Would Donna be shocked or repulsed—or worse yet, scared of him?

Would she see him as a monster?

Maybe it would turn her on.

Just the thought made him hard again.

As if reading his mind, Donna whispered, "I have a confession to make."

Maybe the timing was right after all.

To face her, he raised up on an elbow. "So do I."

"Trust me on this, I should go first." She lifted her eyes to meet his. "Carl, I'm…we're pregnant. The doctor confirmed it yesterday, but I wanted to wait until you got home, so that I could tell you in person. I'm seven weeks along—"

He couldn't remember what she said after that. Her words were drowned out by the wave of joy washing over him. When it subsided, he realized he was stranded on the barren reality of his dual existence.

"Honey, are you alright?" She took his hand in hers. "I know this pregnancy wasn't planned, but we'd always talked of having three children—"

He silenced her with a kiss.

Then with another.

Soon she was crying and laughing at the same time.

She led him back inside her. This time, there was an urgency–no, more like a savagery to their lovemaking.

As they climaxed in each other's arms, it dawned on him that she could never know the truth. Even if he tried to level with her, she wouldn't believe him.

And deep down in his heart, he knew if she did believe him, she could never love him. How could she love a killer?

She couldn't. Case closed.

Maybe it was for the best. If being in his line of work had taught him anything, it was that life was fleeting, so live it well, and hold onto what you have with both fists.

A hard man, in particular, always had a target on his back. During a hit, anything could go wrong, and usually something did. This last trip was a perfect example.

Granted, when it came to covering his tracks, Carl was second to none. He had to be. Otherwise, he'd have to kiss the best part of his two worlds goodbye—the universe filled with the love of Donna, Mary, and Jeff.

But now Donna had given him yet one more reason to stay alive at all costs.

The thought of losing the world they'd built together was all the incentive he needed to keep his mouth shut, and to busy himself with the next best thing: enjoying the precious time they shared.

Donna was surprised when his trigger finger found her, once again.

When she came, she gave that gasp that reminded him of the sound his targets made as they died.

Not that he could ever tell her that.

There are just some things you have to keep to yourself.

CARL'S PHONE WAS BUZZING.

It was a stupid move on his part—leaving it on his

bureau, and still turned on, no less. Until now, he'd never forgotten to turn it off the minute he came home.

At first, he didn't hear it. He'd just gotten out of a hot steamy shower and was scrutinizing the bruises he'd earned while raising Fat Ass onto the toilet. By the time he opened the bathroom door, it was too late. Donna, who had been brushing her hair in front of the bedroom mirror, instinctively reached over and picked up his cell.

A second later, Carl was at her side—close enough to hear the man on the other end of the line chattering away in German.

Donna was so amazed that she was at a loss for words. The man at the other end of the line must have realized this because he paused, then uttered in perfect English, "Simon? Are you there, Simon?"

"No, there is no Simon here," Donna said firmly. "You have the wrong number."

The deathly silence between them was finally broken when, in perfect English, the man asked ever so politely, "Tell me, who owns this phone?"

Before Donna could answer him, Carl plucked the cell out of her hand and disconnected the call.

She teared up, but didn't say anything.

He felt her eyes follow him back to the bathroom, where he closed the door behind him. He knew his actions seemed cruel to her. He knew he should put on his game face and say something, but he was too shocked to think through a plausible lie as to why some German person was calling his cell and asking for him as "Simon," let alone why it should have rattled him in the first place.

Simon was the alias he'd used in his dealings with the Quorum.

He had recognized the voice on the other end of the phone as that of his Quorum handler, Eric Weber.

He'd never given Eric his cell number.

Something was terribly wrong.

He had every right to be scared.

At that moment, he knew exactly what he had to do: *play for time.*

He waited a half hour. When he opened the door, the lights were off.

Donna was sound asleep.

He took the cell phone with him. After slipping downstairs and out the front door, he jogged down the block to an overlook perched above the traffic flowing up and down the Pacific Coast Highway. When he was sure he was alone, he dialed his client's number.

Eric must have recognized his cell because he didn't bother with the formalities in greeting the man he knew as Simon by name. "I'm surprised you called back," he said in English.

"Why wouldn't I?" Carl replied in perfect German. "I took care of the Canadian problem."

"You were sloppy." Eric's tone sent a chill down Carl's spine. "You can imagine our surprise when our contact in the Canadian Security Intelligence Service informed us of your affiliation with Acme Industries."

With that statement, there went the hope Carl may have had that he hadn't blown his cover.

"We presumed you were following our orders. But I see now how it might work in Acme's favor as well. One of their clients is your neighbor to the north, *ja*? You've now rid it of a traitor. Talk about killing two birds with one stone." Eric chuckled. "For a family man to take on such an assignment —to go under deep cover with a group such as the Quorum —you're either very brave, or very stupid. Which is it, Mr. Stone? No need to answer. We both know the question has no merit to your future—or that of your family's."

"You're writing me off too soon, Eric," Carl muttered.

"You'll have to convince me otherwise." The response was glib, yet Carl knew Eric too well. He was dead serious. "And at this stage, Mr. Stone, our trust comes at a very steep price. You've got less than twenty-four hours to make us an offer that proves your loyalty, once and for all."

The line went dead.

Carl walked back into the house, but he couldn't go to bed.

He stayed up all night, until the plan came to him—how he would buy himself time with the Quorum.

How he could escape, when the time came.

What he would give up, so that he could protect his family.

When Donna rose at sunrise, she found him staring out the window.

He walked over to her. His kiss said it all: *Forgive me, please.*

He knew she had when she brought his palm to her cheek. "Always and forever," she whispered.

Always and forever, he vowed.

WHAT CARL DANGLED IN FRONT OF THE QUORUM WAS INDEED something they couldn't refuse.

However, it would come at a very high price for Carl.

But should he deliver, the Quorum would need him more than ever.

Carl knew this was obvious to Eric, too, because of the way the German laughed raucously, even as he tapped Carl's mug of *glühwein* with his own.

It was early evening. They were standing dead center in one of Cologne, Germany's renowned kriskindlemarts. This particular open air Christmas market was the busiest in the city because it took place in a plaza that flanked the Dom, the city's grandest cathedral and one of its most notable attractions.

The time and place of their rendezvous was both a curse and a blessing. Carl had no illusions that Eric had come alone. If he hadn't liked what Carl had to offer, Carl would not make it out of the plaza alive. No doubt there was a sharpshooter or two scoping him from a window high in one of the buildings circling the market, if not from one of the shadowy corners in the cathedral's steeply pitched roof. Even if a bullet missed him, he could easily be knifed while maneuvering through the thick crowd.

Eric didn't ask how Carl would get his hands on the item in question. A bigger issue was when—and the sooner, the better.

"It will take some time," Carl conceded. Not that he wanted Eric to know it, but if he were to cover his tracks, he'd have to move slowly.

"You have six months," Eric warned Carl. He sipped the last of his hot mulled wine, left his mug on the slim waist-high counter between them, and slipped away into the throng of holiday revelers.

Carl was relieved, but he knew he hadn't bought himself much time. More to the point, he hated the fact that by then, Donna would be near her due date. Still, if everything worked out as he planned, by then what the Quorum wanted wouldn't matter.

And what he wanted in return would certainly be within reach.

Until then, the success of every mission assigned to him —by both Acme and the Quorum—was crucial.

In the meantime, he had to secure the safety of his family.

Which meant keeping his situation to himself, at all costs.

RYAN CLANCY PRESUMED THAT CARL'S TENACITY WAS compensation for the Canadian mission's hiccup. Since then, the intel he provided Acme about the Quorum was solid gold.

Ryan didn't know it, but this was only because Carl had to keep playing both ends against the middle until his plan was in place. The stuff being fed was actually chicken feed— genuine enough, but nothing of earthshaking importance, mostly disinformation and intel on the organization's discarded assets. Typical of most terrorist organizations, the Quorum had a high burn rate anyway.

Still, Acme showed Carl its appreciation with a much-deserved raise. It provided a down payment for a spacious mock-Tudor in Hilldale, an exclusive planned community in Orange County, just south of Los Angeles.

When Donna saw all that Hilldale had to offer—the spacious lots, a country club, its very own "village square" with a gourmet grocery and upscale retail shops—she couldn't believe he was serious. "It's a big financial leap for us, what with the baby on the way, and all," she said doubtfully as she patted her belly. "I mean, it certainly is beautiful. And the schools here are incredible! Still...well, I'd feel guilty about the commute you'd have to make every day–"

But Carl had already made up his mind: the house was going to be theirs. The telltale sign of this was the cocky tilt of his head. "Don't feel guilty, ever, because I've earned it—the hard way. Believe me."

For just a second, Carl's satisfied grin was replaced by a hard grimace. "This promotion means more extended business trips. That's part of my new deal. Don't I deserve a palace to come home to?"

My new deal.

She'd never really know the terms of that deal—or with whom it was made.

From the wary look on Donna's face, he could tell she was still uncomfortable with the idea of this new house. So to keep from arguing about it in front of the children, Carl scooped up Jeff and tossed him over his shoulder.

Their son squealed with delight.

"My turn, Daddy! My turn!" Mary jumped down out of the tree house in the broad heritage oak, which she had already claimed as her own. Wrapping her arms around Carl's knees, all three tumbled to the ground, laughing.

"See, babe? This is the American dream, right? This is what it's all about."

2

Raven

In the world of espionage, the term "sparrow" is used to describe a female agent whose job is to entrap a potential asset, or acquire necessary intel, by any means possible, including seduction.

Male agents may also use sex as a means of accomplishing the mission at hand.

It's a dirty job, but someone has to do it.

"Are you someone I should know?" The woman—tall, willowy slim with dark auburn hair, exquisite cheekbones, and an aristocratic British accent—wasn't smiling, but there was a hint of flirtatiousness in her tone.

The yacht glided gently yet swiftly over Venice's Grand Canal. Despite the fact that the sun had already melted into the horizon, the woman did not remove her sunglasses, making it all the more difficult for him to know for sure if she was coming on to him.

There was enough of a breeze that she held onto her large floppy hat with one hand. It was the exact shade of turquoise as her strapless sundress.

Jack Craig wondered if her eyes were also that hue.

On the other hand, by the way in which she rolled her tongue slowly over her full parted lips, he'd be willing to bet all the chips he'd won last night on the blackjack table at *Ca 'Vendramin Calergi* that he could have her, right then and there. It was film festival time in Venice, so anything was possible—especially on a yacht headed to an after-party celebrating the opening night screening of the most talked-about documentary of this year's selections, *Sparks Fly*.

Smiling down at her, he murmured, "No, sorry. I'm just along for the ride."

Just at that moment, Jack caught the eye of the yacht's owner—the film's producer, Ross Tanner. He'd obviously heard their little tête-a-tête because he roared with laughter. "Don't believe him, Rebecca. Mr. Craig is the reason Leonid is throwing this little shindig. We're trying to coax him into financing the sequel to *Sparks Fly*."

Jack, Ross, and the sublimely attractive Rebecca were just three of the beautiful people on the boat headed to Palazzino Alvisi, a historic estate fronting the Grand Canal. For the duration of the festival, it had been leased by Ross's producing partner—Leonid Romanov, the son of a Russian industrialist worth around sixteen billion dollars, whose contracts with his country's state-owned oil company made him the world's richest oil trader.

Jack presumed Rebecca was an actress, like the other women on the yacht. She certainly looked familiar, but he didn't go to enough movies to be certain.

"Ah! The moneymen are circling, like flies. I hope you're willing to make a generous offer," Rebecca nodded toward a fussy little man standing on the starboard side of the boat. He squinted at the water, not through tinted frames, but through round horn-rimmed glasses. Whereas most of the men were casually attired in slacks and open-necked shirts under blazers, the man wore a wool suit, and his neck was noosed in a thin tie. One odd little vanity was a ring, which the man wore on his pinky finger—gold, with a flat black onyx stone adorned with some sort of design in gold filigree.

It's the number, '13,' Jack realized.

The waves slapping against the boat were gentle, so there was no reason for the man to be ill. Still, his complexion was pale, and he was uncomfortable enough that he patted the back of his neck with a handkerchief.

An angelic smile lit Rebecca's face. "Perhaps you should take me with you when you negotiate. I can be a good luck charm, you know."

Jack smiled, but added firmly, "Thanks for the offer, but I'll have to pass. I've heard that Mr. Romanov is easily distracted in the presence of beautiful women. This is one time I need his undivided attention."

Her pout would have been more believable if it hadn't come so swiftly on the heels of a sly smile.

It won her a wider grin, but no concession from Jack. The last thing he needed was to be chased all night by some starlet with an ambitious agenda. He had his own end game:

Steal a thumb drive from their host that contained a list of Russian Prime Minister Vladimir Putin's offshore bank account numbers and passwords.

When briefing Jack about this mission, Ryan Clancy,

Jack's boss at Acme Industries, made no bones about why it was important that he succeed.

"For fifteen years, the US has been trying to follow the money. This is our big break. With this intel, the US will be able to freeze Putin's assets based on current sanctions our country and the UN have placed against Russia. Even more importantly, public knowledge of how Russia's prime minister has skimmed from his country's coffers may be the call-to-arms the Russian people need."

"How did Leonid get ahold of the account list?" Jack asked.

"Boris Romanov, Leonid's father, is one of only five men in Putin's inner circle. This illustrious group got the pick of Russia's plum businesses—it's oil, transportation and financial services. Lucky Boris refines all of Russia's oil reserves. In return, these men provide hidden kickbacks, all of which filter into various hidden bank accounts that are managed by Boris. By now, Putin's piggy bank is estimated at over fifty billion dollars. And it's not just cash, either. Other assets include mansions, cars, planes, helicopters—you name it." Ryan shrugged. "But Boris was recently diagnosed with terminal cancer. Leonid is being groomed to take over the business, which is why Boris gave him a copy of the account list on a thumb drive."

Jack shrugged. "I imagine an active CEO of something as important as Romanov Corporation wouldn't have time to dabble in filmmaking, let alone enjoy the perks that come with it—the photo ops with actors, walking the red carpet at the film festivals, and an endless cavalcade of starlets through his bedroom."

Ryan nodded. "You're right. Leonid is not too keen on

this turn of events, since it'll make a dent in his very active social life. On the other hand, Leonid's wife, Irina, would certainly appreciate this change. Reliable sources tell us that his latest infatuation is Tatyana Zakharov, the Russian operative who works for the Quorum, an organization that finances terrorist cells. Acme has an agent or two who've been tracking it for quite some time now."

Jack shrugged. "I guess someone has to foot the bill for all those jihadist camps."

"Trust me, the Quorum does much more than that. From the intel we've gathered so far, its leaders are well financed, well connected, and well hidden from public view. But even the Quorum would appreciate a windfall, if it fell into their laps. Apparently, the organization also has its eyes on Putin's private cash stash. Tatyana must not have delivered the goods yet, because she's still very much Leonid's current arm charm."

"So, I'll finally get to meet the Quorum's infamous sparrow." Jack was up for a Tatyana sighting, if only out of professional curiosity.

"I doubt it, since Irina is also in Venice and will certainly be attending the party. Leonid may be an egotist, but even he isn't bold enough to flaunt his latest dalliance in her presence. Irina's father was the last director of what we quaintly remember as the KGB. Why tempt a family feud?"

Ryan handed Jack a photo. Irina Romanov was a square-jawed, thin-lipped woman in her early forties. The gray suit she wore in the picture did nothing to enhance a full body that was soft, but not plump. Her dark brown hair was pulled back from her face in a French twist.

"Any suggestions on where I might find the thumb drive?" Jack asked.

"Except when he's walking the red carpet, Romanov keeps an aluminum attaché case with him at all times. During his stay in Venice, the best guess is that it's kept in his private office at Palazzino Alvisi. At some point in the evening, you'll have your meeting with him and his co-producer, Ross Tanner, to offer financing terms for the film. More than likely, the meeting will take place there. It will give you a chance to scope it out, and to return when you know it's empty. You'll be working solo, but our new tech op, Arnie Locklear, has a couple of toys for you to take with you."

Arnie shook Jack's hand vigorously. "I've already sent you a schematic of the villa, which you can easily memorize. The office has a safe large enough to hold an attaché case. You'll find it behind a framed poster of the movie *Tart and Sour*, which Romanov produced as well. It opens with a retinal scan."

"Then how will I open it?"

"Easy. Just take a selfie of you and Leonid, with this." He handed Jack an iPhone. "The camera is equipped with pattern-capturing software that will reproduce his irises exactly. Just point the picture at the color dot, and you'll be in the safe in no time."

"Ryan, why a thumb drive? Why not place the intel in a secure cloud instead?" Jack asked.

"Putin isn't just grousing for the cameras when he declares the Internet has been a CIA project from its inception. He rightly believes that Russia is under American scrutiny at all times."

Ryan glanced at Jack's intricately carved platinum band. "Leave it on. Your cover includes your marriage."

Jack winced. He hadn't broken the news to Ryan that, recently, his wife of two years had left him—the first of many relationships to crumble under the strain of a stressful job that took him all over the world and bound him to secrecy.

Just this morning, when he discovered she'd taken the square ebony box holding those things dearest to him, he made the decision to remove the ring.

How ironic, he thought now.

Apparently, ambitious actresses aren't sentimental either. While the deck hands scurried to secure the yacht among the others tethered to Palazzino Alvisi's massive dock, Rebecca removed her sunglasses in order to better admire his wedding band. At the same time, Jack had a first glance at her eyes—almond-shaped, hard and bright, like well-cut sapphires. "Ah! Your wife has wonderful taste."

Any hope Jack may have had that knowledge of a spouse would dampen her enthusiasm disappeared once and for all when she brushed past him while descending the boarding ramp. Even if her frock hadn't been made of sheer silk, he'd have felt her hardened nipples against his jacket.

Great, thought Jack, the last thing I need is my very own shadow. So that she takes the hint, I'll give her the cold shoulder the moment we get inside so that she realizes I'm not up for any fun and games.

The sooner he met with Leonid, the better.

JACK'S INTRODUCTION TO HIS HOST HAPPENED TOO LATE IN THE evening—almost at the party's conclusion.

Worse yet, it was too short and not so sweet. Leonid's breath smelled of vodka, he barely smiled, and his eyes roamed to the other guests even as Jack assured him that he was eager to talk about the sequel's financing. A very broad hint that serious face time wasn't going to happen came with a slap on the back and a promise to "discuss the project in a more conducive setting. Let's say lunch, tomorrow on the terrace at Lineadombra?"

Jack nodded and smiled benignly. Holding up Arnie's iPhone, he said, "Do you mind? The wife will kill me if I don't get a picture of me with her favorite producer."

Leonid shrugged, but Jack knew he was flattered by the smirk he gave when the cell phone's camera clicked. Afterward Tanner hustled Leonid in the direction of an aging American action star.

Good riddance, Jack thought.

He shifted his gaze to the mezzanine. Which room was the office, he wondered. Oh yes, it was the second of two double doors located directly across from the large staircase that connected the two lower floors.

As his eyes moved across the second story's open hall, they rested on a solitary figure: Irina Romanov.

She was leaning over the ornate wrought-iron railing that circled the mezzanine, frowning down at the crowd below.

Unlike the other ladies in attendance, she was not adept at the sleight of hand that allowed more determined women to feign fleeting youth. Neither was she as stylish as her female guests. Her widow's peak was already graying. A few stray tendrils had escaped her chignon. Her black cocktail dress hugged her solid frame in all the wrong places.

There were tears in her eyes.

In fact, her eyeliner was smudged to the point where black streaks darkened the webs of fine lines attached to the corners of her eyes.

Had Tatyana Zakharov shown up anyway?

The only picture Acme had of the Russian agent was at least two years old. It had been taken off a street security webcam feed in Istanbul. Jack cursed himself for not having scrutinized it better, not that it would have mattered. She'd worn oversized sunglasses, and the picture was in black and white. She wore a scarf over her head, but from what he could see of her hair peeking out over her forehead, she was a platinum blonde. Then again, as with all agents, male or female, she may have been wearing a wig.

He scanned the faces of the two hundred guests milling below them in the grand ballroom. All night long, Ross and Leonid had been shaking hands with the film's fans and well-wishers. At this very moment, beside the nervous little man from the boat, at least four comely beauties were hanging on Leonid's every word. The women were not shy in their attempts to provoke the producer, and he was not at all bashful in returning their admiration with a wink, or for that matter a forthright proposition.

And Jack wasn't at all surprised to see that Rebecca was one of Leonid's ardent acolytes. Tatyana didn't have to be here for Irina Romanov to see her husband in action. She was a producer's wife. Thanks to his movies and the prizes they'd garnered for him, he was a celebrity.

The groupies followed. Temptation was inevitable.

So was a wife's heartache.

Especially that of a wife as humble and homely as Irina Romanov.

As sorry as he felt for her, he knew there was nothing he could do about it. In fact, Leonid's vanity worked to his favor.

He watched as she made her way toward the staircase. But instead of joining the party, she walked up to the third story.

Smart woman, he thought.

Now that the second story was clear, he slipped up the back stairwell.

THE ATTACHÉ CASE WASN'T ANYWHERE IN THE OFFICE.

Not in or around the massive Baroque desk, or stuck in any of the floor-to-ceiling bookcases.

And while he got into the safe with no problem at all, it was empty, except for a pair of platinum diamond-studded cufflinks.

Jack couldn't find anything resembling a thumb drive in any of the desk drawers, either.

Where the hell was it?

The master bedroom was next door.

It couldn't hurt to look there as well.

BY USING THE TERRACE, HE MADE IT OUT ONE SET OF DOUBLE-paneled doors and into the other without anyone seeing him.

Roused by the gentle breeze coming through the open balcony doors, the white gauze curtains rose and snapped like waking wraiths. What little light there was in the room came in from the lampposts lining the Grand Canal below.

In fact, the room was so dark that Jack hadn't noticed the woman lying on the high four-poster bed until she rose onto her elbows.

It was Irina Romanov.

Jack made sure that none of his dismay on her behalf was reflected in his eyes. "Ah, Mrs. Romanov! I—I guess I'm in the wrong room. I was summoned to your husband's office." He held out his hand. "It's good to finally meet you. I'm Jack Craig, with Acme Industries' Financial Securities division."

She stared down as she replied, "Yes, I know your name. You're the banker interested in financing the sequel to Leonid's latest and greatest." Finally, she took his hand and shook it limply. "Let me guess. Leonid—how do you Americans say it? Oh yes—he blew you up."

Jack shrugged. "What you mean to say is that he blew me *off.*"

As if confirming her supposition, Leonid's laughter rose over the din of the crowd, now standing down by the dock at the water's edge.

The party was over and Jack had failed.

Seeing the look of disgust on his face, Irina shrugged. "I hope I did not sound too rude. What I say is a reflection of my own experience with my husband. He has his priorities, sometimes to the detriment of those who can do him the most good."

"Have I wrongly presumed that the financing of his next film is his current focus?"

"His priorities change with the wind. One day, his quest is an Oscar. Another day, it is notoriety, fame, and celebrity —even if it means funding pornography." She shrugged as she rose from the bed. "As with most ambitious men, next on his list is another sexual conquest. My Leonid has no true loyalty, with principles or people." Ashamed, she looked down at her feet. "He does not even have a love of country."

She knows about the Putin payoffs, Jack realized.

He tilted her head up, so that she had to look him in the eye.

Then, very gently, he kissed her lips.

She didn't recoil, or even blush, let alone back away.

Instead, she savored it.

She fell into the kiss, and into his arms.

Afterward she whispered, "I cannot influence him, if that is what you want of me."

To dissuade her from this presumption, he placed his index finger on her cheek and let it roam diagonally to her lips.

She sucked it in between her teeth—slowly, at first, but then she nipped it hungrily.

He pushed her back down onto the bed.

"No..." Her voice sounded so far away, but she didn't fight him when he raised her arms, pinning them over her head with one hand while the other cupped her left breast. She closed her eyes and moaned softly when he squeezed her nipple gently between his index and third fingers.

Then she looked down and noticed the ring on his

wedding finger. He felt her stiffen. "So, you are married." Her tone was listless.

Damn it, he thought. Still, his cover was rock solid. He had to go with it. "Yes." At the very least, he sounded penitent.

It wasn't part of any act. What woman wants a man who won't tell her where he goes at night, or for that matter weeks on end? What woman isn't pained at the scent of another on the man she loves deeply?

All women are, and this woman was no exception, he knew.

Irina wrenched her hands from his grip—

But only to unclasp his belt buckle.

She did not stop him when he lifted her skirt and entered her.

His thrusts were relentless. She closed her eyes and bit her lips, whispering her groans into his ear.

He felt her climax, and he knew she felt his surge as well.

They collapsed in each other's arms.

She started to sob.

"Please don't cry," he murmured.

"I always weep when I am happy," she whispered back. She rose from the bed and turned to face the large ornate mirror over the dresser. She sighed at what she saw. Her hair had fallen out of the twist, and her eyes were black with mascara.

At least the lipstick was gone from her teeth.

She slipped on a pair of plain black low-heeled pumps then she smoothed her dress back into place. She didn't bother to tame the errant strands of hair that had escaped her French twist. Instead, she plucked the last of the pins that held it in place, so that the rest of her thick, curly mane fell in loose coils below her rounded shoulders.

She didn't look at him but into the mirror as she dabbed the smudges under her eyes with a tissue. "Mr. Craig, I meant what I said. I have absolutely no influence over Leonid."

"I didn't make love to you because of him."

She paused, then shrugged. "It's very kind of you to say so. But I'm a realist. And more importantly, I am grateful." She turned to him—not to look him in the eye, but to touch the ring on his finger. "Your wife is a very lucky woman."

He started to speak again, but before he could get a word out, she put a finger against his lips to quiet him. "On the other hand, I am married to a monster. Not just I, but too many of my countrywomen have discovered this the hard way."

"What do you mean by that?"

"Pornography keeps my husband's film company in the black." She turned back to the mirror and patted away her tears. "So you see, meeting with him now is a waste of your time, and your company's money. Once word gets out about my husband's exploits—and eventually, it will—he will be, how do you say, an industry pariah."

Jack frowned. "Even if the public were to discover this shadow business, why would it turn against him?"

"Because of the way in which his 'stars' are procured for his projects. Most are real actresses. Leonid promises them the stardom they seek at all costs. Instead, once they are on the locked set, they find out the truth about their new film role. If they scream or fight back, they are drugged before the filmed rapes begin." Irina shivered. "This filth gets millions of downloads, but the girls are never seen or heard from again. I presume they're sold into prostitution afterward—or worse. I've seen one of these films." Irina's lower lip trembled. "Today, he will have many women to choose from. No doubt his auditions have already begun. Later tonight, after the rest of the guests have left, his 'chosen ones' will be asked to stay behind."

"Would you like my help in stopping him?"

She looked over at him. "Yes, of course!"

"Then I'll need your help, too."

She nodded. "Anything."

"Irina, Leonid carries an attaché case, given to him by his father."

She shrugged. "I know it, yes. He hates it! He says he's not a businessman—that he is an artist, a creative genius. Ha! He may feel his father's money makes him both, but neither is close to the truth."

"The case contains something that will implicate him in this and other crimes. It wasn't in his office. Do you have any idea where is it now?"

Irina stepped over to the floor-to-ceiling bookcase. The fourth shelf from the bottom held a leather-bound series of Charles Dickens novels. She tilted the one entitled *Bleak House*. Eight other books in the series slid to one side, revealing a safe. Irina tapped eight numbers on the digital keyboard.

The door opened, revealing the attaché case.

As she handed it to Jack, the books slipped back into place, as if they were never disturbed.

"The clasp has a combination lock. To open it, try eight six zero eight zero two. Most of Leonid's pass codes are the birth date of our son, Alexi." Irina took Jack's hand and stroked it lovingly. "Use all possible caution, Mr. Craig. I'll do the same. Now if you'll excuse me, our guests are outside, taking their leave. I'll do what I can to make sure my husband stays out of your way."

She walked out, closing the door behind her.

To play it safe, Jack watched out the window until she came into view. She'd done a good job in pulling herself together. In fact, now she held her head high, and her shoulders back as she crossed to her husband's side.

Leonid was in the middle of a discussion with some effusive British comedian who had just made his film debut at the festival. Irina inched through the crowd chatting by the water's edge until she reached her husband's side. When he finally noticed her there, he did a double take. Jack couldn't hear what he was saying, but he saw Leonid pointing to her hair and laughing raucously.

She recoiled, as if he'd slapped her across the face.

He shrugged as she walked away, defeated.

The others, chagrined, covered for him with nervous laughter.

"Leonid Romanov, you're incorrigible!" Rebecca teased him.

Jack fought the urge to shoot the bastard right then and there.

Better payback would come with the accomplishment of his mission.

He turned to the task at hand.

Jack nudged the six tumblers to those numbers Irina suggested.

The clasp flipped up, and Jack opened the case.

Inside, there were several folders. Most of them contained documents written in Russian, although one was in German, and another in English.

The top of the case had three pockets of varying sizes. All were empty.

Where the hell was it?

Jack pulled out the folders in order to feel around the bottom and the sides of the case. He was looking for any seam, indentation or lump that might indicate a hidden compartment.

He found a catch on the lid of the case. When he pressed it, a small square hole revealed itself, just deep enough to hold a thin rectangular disk.

The thumb drive.

He grabbed it—

Not a moment too soon. He heard a voice on the other side of the door. It belonged to Leonid.

But he wasn't alone. From the woman's laugh, Jack knew his host was nowhere near the party's hostess.

Leonid was with the actress, Rebecca.

There was nowhere to go but under the bed.

"Really, Leonid, I don't think we should do this now, and certainly not here—I mean, with your wife downstairs and all." Rebecca's words expressed wariness, but to Jack's ear, her honeyed tone seemed ripe with anticipation.

Leonid's response was much as Jack's would have been, had he been the one to coerce Rebecca into his bedroom.

So, she was the one he'd chosen for his next rape film.

As they fell onto the bed, the mattress sagged practically to Jack's face. He could barely breathe, and he certainly couldn't turn his head.

"Leonid, please! I said—I said no!" The slap that followed brought a pause to the action above Jack's head.

But not for long. It was followed by another slap.

And then a deep moan.

Was Leonid hurting her?

"I told you, Leonid—I'm not into the rough stuff." Rebecca's warning was serene, not angry or frightened. Jack presumed she was trying not to panic.

"My dear Rebecca, you also said you'd make an exception in my case." Leonid's tone was firm. "Look what I have, just for you—the handcuffs you were admiring, just the other day."

"You're mistaken. If anyone was admiring them, it was you." This time, Rebecca's tone was as cold as ice.

"Indulge me," Leonid insisted.

The next sound—that of the sharp click of metal upon metal.

"It's...too tight," Rebecca murmured.

"You'll see. You'll like it that way." Leonid laughed. "I know I will."

He didn't waste any time proving this boast. With each thrust, the mattress groaned and dipped. Jack flattened his head against the floor.

I hope this asshole comes quickly, Jack thought. Otherwise, I may suffocate.

He took the gamble of tilting his head to one side, where he could see out the door to the balcony. While they're preoccupied, he thought, maybe I could inch my way out from under here and crawl out onto the patio, then down onto the Grand Canal's promenade.

He was just about to make a move in that direction when he saw a pair of feet in the threshold of the balcony door:

Low-heeled, plain black pumps.

Irina.

Jack could only imagine the look of horror on her face.

What he couldn't imagine was what she'd do next.

The gun must have had a suppressor because Jack barely heard the whisking bullet leaving the chamber. On the other hand, its target gave a loud gasp. The thump that followed was proof that Irina's shot had hit its mark.

In no time, Jack was on his feet.

Irina stood frozen, staring at the bed where the gun was aimed.

Jack was not shocked to see that the victim was Leonid. The bullet caught him on the left side of his neck. There was so much blood that it was obvious she'd struck his carotid artery.

What did surprise him was that it was Leonid who had been handcuffed to the bedposts.

Rebecca was sitting on top of the dead man. Realizing the gun was pointed her way, her eyes narrowed warily. "Please, Mrs. Romanov, put down the gun."

Instead Irina shifted her aim to Rebecca. "You slut! If it hadn't been for you—"

"Irina, hand it to me." Jack kept his voice gentle, but firm.

"No! You don't understand—"

A second later, Rebecca was off the bed and beside Irina.

Before Jack could react, she elbowed the older woman in the stomach. As Irina doubled over, Rebecca wrenched the gun out of her hand and pointed it back at her.

Jack stared at her. "Whoa, Rebecca, it's okay. You're safe now."

She smiled as she shot him in the shoulder.

"What the hell!" Jack shouted. Irina muffled a scream with a hand over her mouth.

Rebecca motioned to Irina. "*Gde portfel?*" she asked.

Jack recognized the language. She'd asked in Russian, *Where is the briefcase?*

"Who the hell are you?" he asked.

She swung the gun around so that it was up against Jack's temple. Pressing her lips into a pout, she murmured, "I don't know if I should be proud of the fact that I've so successfully deceived the celebrated Acme operative Jack Craig, or disappointed that you obviously don't sleep with my picture under your pillow."

"Tatyana Zakharov is...*was* my husband's latest whore," Irina muttered.

Well, Jack thought, that explains a lot, including why she's about to blow my head off.

"Your husband had something I wanted," Tatyana continued, this time in Russian. "A computer memory stick."

Irina's eyes shifted to Jack involuntarily.

Seeing this, Tatyana smiled. In English, she purred, "Ah, I see. You sweet-talked this old bat into fetching it for you." She slapped the gun against his temple. "Hand it over."

Jack was attempting to staunch the blood from his shoulder wound with his left hand. Slowly, he lowered his right one into his pocket and pulled out the thumb drive. He held it out to her—

When she reached for it he tossed his arm over his shoulder and muttered, *"Plavat' za eto, suka."*

Translation: *Swim for it, bitch.*

They heard the *ker-plop* through the balcony window.

Tatyana let loose with an angry shriek. But this time, when she raised her gun to shoot Jack, Irina grabbed the younger woman's arm. They struggled. Just as Irina yanked it from Tatyana's hand, the gun went off.

Irina gasped and looked down.

Blood gushed from her chest.

She fell backward—out the window, with the gun.

This time, the splash they heard was louder.

Angered, Tatyana stalked back to the bed. She rummaged in the bloodied sheets until she came up with her purse, from which she pulled a cell phone. She hit a button, waited, then said, "Mission aborted. Wait for me by the dock."

So, she had an accomplice, Jack thought. Was it Ross Tanner?

She reached down for her stilettoes. As she strapped them on, she bent down so that she and Jack were face-to-face. "The nearest hospital is *Servizio Citta'Di Rosin Massimo.* It's, oh say, a ten-minute walk from here. Since you'll probably bleed out on the way, here's a little something to remember me by."

She gave him an open-mouthed kiss.

"Not bad," she murmured.

She walked down the terrace steps without a backward look.

He didn't wait until the click of her heels echoed on the slate steps to start crawling out.

He saw her run onto the dock, where Ross Tanner's boat was waiting. When Ross saw her, he started the engine.

The fussy little man with the pinky ring helped her climb onboard.

So, they're Quorum operatives, too, Jack thought.

He groaned in pain as he shifted his shoulder in order to reach the gun in his back holster.

The boat's engine had already started when the bullet hit its mark, but his aim was off. It wasn't Tatyana who fell forward in the boat but Ross.

Was he dead? Jack couldn't tell.

He would have preferred that the shocked look on Tatyana's face was from the pain of a second bullet, but he was too weak to get off another shot. Realizing her luck, she smiled triumphantly back at him.

Pinky Ring stumbled to the boat's steering wheel. After a lurch forward, the boat sped off in the dead of night.

JACK WAS SO WEAK THAT HE CRAWLED ONLY AS FAR AS THE dock. There, he collapsed beside a skiff.

Later, he learned he had been saved by a couple who had walked down to the self-service rialto for a bowl of calamari. If the husband hadn't come back to the boat to fetch a shawl for his wife, Jack would have bled to death. He staunched the wound with the shawl while she steered the skiff to the hospital.

JACK AWOKE TO FIND HIS WOUND DRESSED. HE WAS IN A hospital gown. When he rang for the nurse, she was able to tell him in broken English that although his jacket and shirt had been too bloody to keep, his pants had been saved.

Jack let loose with a relieved sigh. *"I miei pantaloni, pronto per favore."*

He had to get the pants back. The thumb drive was still in the pocket.

It was his wedding ring he'd tossed out the window instead.

The nurse hurried out. When she came back, she had a paper bag with her.

Inside were his pants, neatly folded. In the pocket was the thumb drive. His wallet was also there. Nothing had been taken from it.

When the nurse left to get on with her duties, he crumpled the empty bag and tossed it across the room.

He put on his pants and slipped out of the hospital, shirtless.

He stopped at the first store he could to buy a T-shirt. The only ones they had were emblazoned with:

VENICE IS FOR LOVERS

It would have to do for now.

He had to run to catch the next flight to Charles de Gaulle Airport. Tired and still aching from his shoulder wound, he dropped into his seat and immediately closed his eyes, hoping to get some sleep during the two-hour flight to Paris.

As he drifted off, he saw Irina's face—her sad eyes and sweet smile. She hadn't deserved to die that way.

And she certainly hadn't deserved the spouse she had been cursed with.

Neither do I, Jack thought. Good riddance to her.

"YOU LOOK LIKE SHIT," CARL STONE MUTTERED TO JACK.

They were sitting across from each other in the VIP lounge at CDG. Jack had just received notice from Acme that he was to hand off Leonid's thumb drive to Carl, who was flying home to LAX after some hijinks of his own.

"Thanks. Great to see you, too." Jack winced as he moved his shoulder to position it a bit more comfortably. The thumb drive was folded into the Technology section of that day's edition of *The Wall Street Journal,* which Jack had just laid on the coffee table between them.

When a cocktail waitress came over to drop off his Scotch whiskey, she batted her eyes.

Carl grinned and tipped big.

She walked away without even a glance at Jack.

Noting this, Carl laughed. "You know, guy, you'd have a better chance at getting laid if you lost the tourist T-shirt." Before Jack could retort, Carl added, "Just kidding! Speaking of the old ball and chain—or maybe I should say, having your balls chained—how's married life treating you?"

So that he wouldn't have to go into the pathetic details of

yet another spy's marriage hitting the rocks, Jack countered, "Hey, did I hear you just had another kid?"

Most expectant fathers, Jack knew, could talk about their offspring for hours on end. Jack figured all he had to do was listen and nod for the next fifteen minutes before Carl had to leave for his departing flight to LAX.

Jack's question put a big, bright smile Carl's face. "Yeah, the little lady is ready to pop any day now, with our third." He took a sip of his drink, and then placed it on top of the newspaper.

"Boy or girl?" Jack asked.

"Since we already have one of each, we decided to learn on the tyke's birthday. But I told Donna I'm throwing it in the Pacific Ocean if it's not inclined to pitch a fastball at ninety-seven miles an hour." Carl's eyes never met Jack's because both men were scanning the few others in the lounge to see if anyone was watching. Convinced they were unobserved, Carl picked up his drink, downed it, and slid the newspaper holding the thumb drive under his folded Burberry trench coat.

Just then, a gate update was announced in French by a seductive female voice.

"Your flight is boarding," Jack growled. "Safe journey." Carl held up the Technology section of the paper, as if something important had caught his eye. Then he rose, casually tucking the newspaper under his arm.

Jack didn't move until five minutes after Carl walked out of the lounge.

When he got up to leave, the waitress handed him a note:

Dear Jack, too bad about the ring. I hope it wasn't too great a loss.

Tatyana

Oh, shit, he thought. *So she knows I held onto the thumb drive. She must have followed me to the VIP lounge and seen that the ring was off my finger—*

She must have seen the hand-off to Carl, too.

He ran out the door, and walked as quickly as he could to the airport's architecturally renowned nest of clear escalator tubes. Each ascended or descended from the main terminal to a cluster of boarding gates. Jack had to make sure Carl made his flight, as opposed to lying in some restroom with his jugular slit.

As Jack ascended in one of the tubes, he glanced over to another tube on his right, which was descending from where he was headed.

Tatyana was in it.

She was frowning.

At first she didn't see him. When she realized he was staring at her, she forced her lips into a smile.

Then she threw him a kiss.

He didn't know what to make of it.

He shoved his way forward, beyond some of the other travelers, hustling as fast as he could to Carl's gate.

He got there to find that it had already departed. He went up to the ticket agent. "I need to know if a passenger made the flight. His name is Carl Stone."

The woman frowned, unsure if he was worthy of the information, but the distress in his eyes must have convinced her to ignore his idiotic T-shirt.

"*Oui, monsieur*, he made the flight—just barely."

Relief flooded Jack's face. "*Merci*," he murmured.

So, Tatyana hadn't been able to stop Carl.

Jack couldn't wait to get home, to his own bed.

Then he remembered that going home meant sleeping alone.

JACK WOKE UP WITH A START. IT TOOK HIM JUST A SECOND TO remember why:

Having seen Carl Stone, Tatyana could now have one of her people intercept him at LAX.

He looked at the clock on his bed stand. Hell, he'd slept over ten hours! The plane had landed by now. If they'd gotten to Carl, Ryan would want to debrief him as to how and why things had gone so terribly wrong.

It was a call he wasn't looking forward to making, since it would be on top of a long list of bad news he'd have for his boss, especially if he hadn't yet heard about Leonid and Irina's deaths.

The thought of Ryan's reaction made his wound throb. He needed another painkiller.

He opened his bar. A new bottle of Scotch whiskey was waiting for him.

Yep, that would numb the pain.

He started with a full tumbler, and didn't stop until the bottle was empty, which was somewhere around Monte Carlo.

A little sick leave was certainly in order.

3

Ghost Story

[Contents of Donna Stone's overnight bag, reviewed by Acme Analysis Team]

- *1 floor-length terrycloth robe*
- *1 pair of plush slippers*
- *1 silk negligee*
- *1 pair of support stockings*
- *1 small cosmetic bag, filled with various makeup items*
- *1 stuffed animal (Steiff polar bear)*
- *1 toiletry bag, filled with a tube of toothpaste, a toothbrush, facial cleanser, and moisturizer*
- *1 silver heart-shaped locket*
- *2 handwritten notes, which read:*

Dear Baby,
I hope you are a little sister, and not another dumb little brother.
Love, Mary

Dear Baby,
I hope you don't cry too much.
Stay out of my tree house!!!!!!!
JEFF

- *1 miniature GPS tracking device*

"SHE REFUSES TO HAVE HER BABY UNTIL HER HUSBAND COMES back!" The nurse, Allison, was so embarrassed by what she was saying that she whispered it into the doctor's ear.

He groaned. "Give me a break."

"I'm serious!" She nodded toward the pregnant patient, whose moans were low, but constant. "Supposedly he went home for her overnight bag, but he hasn't returned."

The doctor sighed. "When the hell was that?"

He couldn't see the nurse's mouth because she had on her surgical mask, but the way it clung to her lips, it was obvious she was sucking in her breath—something she did whenever she had bad news. "He left four hours ago."

"That's ridiculous! For all we know, he's hitting every bar between here and their house." He rubbed the fatigue from the last six deliveries from his eyes. "Get her prepped."

"No!" The patient shouted from across the room. "Not until...not until my Carl is here at my side!"

The doctor grabbed the clipboard from the hook at the bottom of the woman's bed. According to Donna Stone's chart, she had come in some time around three in the afternoon.

In fact, Allison had been the one to check them into the

hospital's labor-and-delivery floor. Mrs. Stone, big with child, was already breathing through her labor pains, just like they taught in all the Lamaze classes. Allison was surprised the husband wasn't more anxious. To break the ice, she teased him about it.

"This one will be our third," he assured her. "I know the drill."

She chuckled with him, even as she patted Mrs. Stone's sweaty palm. "Ah! Well, then, you're old hands at this. Do you know yet if it's a girl or a boy?"

"No. We want to be surprised. Besides, they're all little bundles of joy, aren't they?"

Together they helped the patient onto the bed. As Allison strapped Donna's arm to the blood pressure pump, Mr. Stone—Carl, as his wife called him—suddenly declared, "Honey, in the rush to get over here, I must have left your overnight bag at the house. Now that you're checked in, I should go back and get it. Don't worry, be back in no time."

He'd kissed her—full on the lips; tenderly, fervently.

As if it might be the last one they'd ever share.

That's when it hit Allison: Mr. Stone wasn't coming back.

On the other hand, the baby would be here any moment now.

Although Donna was offered an epidural immediately, she refused to take it. Now that she was already dilated to nine centimeters, it was too late, despite the fact that she was convulsing from the pain.

Still, Carl was nowhere to be found.

"Your baby is coming, Donna! You have to be prepped for delivery," Allison begged.

Donna's eyes shadowed her shifting emotions—disappointment, anger, concern, and fear—

And finally, resignation.

"Okay," she murmured. "For the baby's sake."

As Allison positioned Donna's knees and pelvis, Donna grasped her hand and whispered, "For Carl not to be here, something must be terribly wrong."

Allison smiled and forced herself to say, "Everything will be alright."

Still, she couldn't help but feel Donna Stone was right.

IN THE DELIVERY ROOM, PAIN TRUMPS ANGER, BUT FEAR TRUMPS pain.

Most importantly, faith trumps death.

The Stone child was in a frank breech and too far down the birth canal for a C-section to be performed. However, the doctor could still position the infant to be pulled out from the mother, depending on her level of distress.

The delivery team worked furiously to do just that. Throughout the process, they monitored the child's and the mother's heartbeats. But then, at the exact moment the infant girl emerged into the world—seven-twelve that evening—the mother's blood pressure dropped precipitously.

Allison attended to the baby while the doctor and the other delivery nurses worked the crash cart until Donna was stabilized.

When she came to, she whispered, "Can I hold my baby?"

Allison tucked the infant into the crook of her arm. "It's a girl."

"Does Carl know?" Even as Donna Stone asked the question, the dread in her eyes showed she already knew the answer.

"I'll wake you the moment he comes in," Allison promised fervently. "In the meantime, you should try to sleep."

Donna looked down at her baby. "Yes, all right." Gently, she handed over the child. "Trisha is her name. He chose it."

"It's beautiful." Allison smiled. "And she is, too."

She put Trisha in the isolette, then administered a light sedative to the infant's mother.

Donna's eyelids fluttered as the drug took effect. Slumber came with a sigh.

After placing the child in the nursery, Allison ran to the emergency room. No one who matched Carl Stone's description had been admitted. A visit to the hospital morgue relieved her of her worst fear—that her premonition was right.

Still, he might be there. Maybe he took the elevator to the main floor, where the hospital's chapel was located. It was worth checking.

The room held two rows of six benches. She always chose the side closest to the window. The light from a lamppost outside hit the stained glass windows, bathing the altar in front of the pews in a kaleidoscope of color. She fell to her knees and prayed—not just for the mother and the child, but for the father, too.

Solace surged over her, if only for a brief moment. Then it

occurred to her that St. Orange was just one of fifty hospitals in the LA metro area—

Each with its own morgue.

She sighed. On her patient's behalf, she'd spend the balance of her shift describing the tall, handsome man to morgue attendees all over Los Angeles in the hope that they, too, would relieve her of her fear.

She didn't see the man in the chapel's last pew until she was practically out the door. He was in his early fifties. What hair he had left was graying. There was a bulkiness to his frame.

He didn't smile at her. Instead, he kept his eyes downcast, as if in prayer.

She wondered what news he'd heard to bring him there.

She said a little prayer for him, too.

DONNA STONE SLEPT THROUGH THE NIGHT.

Since the husband, Carl, never came back, Allison saw no reason to wake her.

Because she was working a double shift, she was there when the patient awakened. She'd just gotten back to the nurses' station after assisting with the delivery of twins when she saw an overnight bag under her desk. The tag on it was marked D STONE - MATERNITY.

A nursing assistant was sifting through patient files. Allison tapped her on the shoulder. "My God! How long has this been here?"

The woman shrugged. "It was there when I came on my shift, so at least since last night."

Shaking her head, Allison grabbed it and hurried to Donna's room.

She was surprised to see the man from the chapel sitting in one of the guest chairs. Donna was awake, but whatever the man said to her had her sobbing.

Allison handed the bag to her. "Sorry," she said sheepishly. "It was left yesterday, at the front desk. I hope you didn't miss it too badly." She knew she sounded silly. It wasn't the bag Donna wanted. It was her husband.

Donna opened the bag. Allison could see the head of a stuffed animal. It looked like a white teddy bear. Donna held it for a moment, brushing its fur with the palm of her hand before placing it in the perambulator beside her sleeping baby.

They were silent as Allison placed a pitcher of fresh water on Donna's bed stand. Afterward she scurried out of the room, but since the door was left open, she could hear Donna's reactions to the news he'd brought her—words and phrases such as, "...But my children should be able to mourn their father..." And, "Okay, Ryan. I'll go along with your little charade..."

So, Carl Stone is dead. Saddened, Allison bowed her head.

A few minutes later, the man left.

Allison noticed he had the teddy bear with him.

What followed—the new mother's brokenhearted sobs—howls, really—brought both Allison and the nursing assistant into the room in a flash. Allison gave her patient a sedative and stayed at her side until she fell back asleep.

Donna grasped Allison's hand and never let go.

When finally she untangled their entwined fingers, Donna murmured, "My life is one big lie."

4

Burn Notice

A covert operative who receives a burn notice is being told in not-so-polite terms that somehow he's screwed up, and therefore his services are no longer needed.

So that there is no mistaking the meaning of this message, usually this notice is delivered with a bullet to the back of the head.

LAST CALL MADE TO ACME AGENT #415'S (DECEASED) *authorized cell phone, 6:43 pm:*

"Carl, please pick up! This has got to be the sixth call I've made to you! The pains are coming every ninety seconds, and the nurse says it should be any moment now. (Soft crying) I don't want to have our baby without you. Please, just—just call to say that you're okay! That you're...alive."

The caller, female, has been verified as that of Agent 415's wife, Donna Stone.

She is also the caller on the six prior calls.

THE SLICK, BLACK PORSCHE CARRERA PULLED UP TO THE HOT Wheels All-Nite Truck Stop sometime after sunset.

Neither of the women on duty had anything better to do than stare out at the driver as he unwound himself from the low-slung sports car.

"Dibs on Hottie," murmured the café's waitress, Jolene Caruthers.

The cook, Beth Patrick, shrugged. "Why? Do you really think he'll actually come in here for a cup of that dishwater that passes for coffee?"

Jolene shrugged. Beth was probably right. In the one-hundred-and-nine-mile stretch between Palm Springs and the Arizona border, the odds were against him doing anything other than swiping his credit card on the high-octane pump and driving on down the road.

The man who emerged from the sports car stretched tall, as if he had all the time in the world. The lamppost hanging over the gas pumps shed enough light on him that it made it easy for the women to scrutinize him.

Both liked what they saw. He was slim but broad-shouldered. His dark suit, which he wore over a bright white button-down shirt, hugged him like a second skin.

Beth leaned over the dinette counter for a better look.

"Now, what do you suppose a man like that does for a living?" she mused out loud.

Jolene smiled. "Women—and lots of them."

She'd love to be welcomed into that club.

Sadly, when he grabbed the nozzle from the high-octane pump, it looked as if she wouldn't have that chance. Jolene sighed. Only patrons paying by cash came inside the café, unless they were hungry enough for a cup of the tepid coffee and a wedge of the three-day-old cherry pie that sat under the glass dome on the counter.

"I'll just bet he's an actor," Beth chattered. "Who else would have a car like that? I'll just bet he's driving back from Phoenix because he's got some movie role waiting for him—"

Suddenly, Jolene realized he was coming their way.

He was hungry for something after all.

His walk was as smooth as silk, like a man who knew what he wanted and always got it. She'd do what she could to make him want her—right here, and right now.

Well, maybe not there on the counter, but a quickie in the ladies' room, say.

It wouldn't be her first time.

In fact, it happened more often these days, since her boob job. The Las Vegas plastic surgeon had suggested that she go for something less "Anna Nicole Smith-esque, and more Scarlett Johansson-like," but Jolene shook her head, declaring, "Nope, I want the most bang for my buck."

She was getting banged a lot, so the proof was in the pudding.

Still, it was a numbers game, and a girl had to have patience.

It looked as if Jolene's patience had finally paid off.

She hissed to Beth, "Don't you have some spuds to chop, or some pans to wash or something?"

Beth knew the drill. Her loud, long sigh said it all: *you owe me.*

Jolene waited until Beth slammed the back door before sliding behind the cash register.

Even before Hottie opened the front door, she dimpled up and thrust out her chest, but she timed a come-hither lick to her pouty smile when their eyes met.

His response—to give her the once-over—had her so flustered that she practically drenched her thong.

He held out a fifty-dollar bill. "I'd like twenty back, small bills."

She nodded casually. But when she took his money, the warmth from his touch surged through her like an electric current.

So that he couldn't see her blush, she stared down as she slipped the bill into the cash register. As she pulled together his change, she murmured, "Our coffee is the best you'll find between the Arizona border and Twentynine Palms. I made it fresh, myself." She caressed the word "fresh" with such longing that he paused to consider the possibilities.

He chuckled, then nodded toward the pie pedestal. "Did you make that yourself, too?"

"Who, little ol' me?" she giggled. There was no way in hell she'd take credit for a Costco pie. Instead, she purred, "I have a lot of talents, but baking ain't one of them."

To help him guess what she excelled at instead, she let her eyes drop to his crotch.

She took her time raising her eyes to meet his. Hottie's deep green eyes were mesmerizing.

She reached out with his change. But this time when their hands touched, he held fast to hers—

In order to pull her even closer.

She shifted her face up so that her lips were just inches away. Her free hand went to his hardened bulge. Oh yeah, he'll do, she thought.

And I am so ready—

Then they heard it: another car, pulling up into the parking lot out front.

Hottie's grin disappeared. His eyes narrowed as he watched the driver get out of the car.

The man was short, bald, and certainly over fifty, from what Jolene could tell. Despite the desert heat, the man wore a jacket over a white shirt and khaki slacks. He paused before entering in order to take off his round-framed spectacles, breathe on the lenses, and wipe them with a handkerchief.

Ah, hell, thought Jolene. The dude has lousy timing.

Hottie nodded toward the corner booth. "You talked me into that coffee and pie."

It pissed her off that he hadn't had time to take her up on her promise for the best sex of his life.

It made her just as angry that Baldy pulled up in the no-parking zone. If an eighteen-wheeler stopped for fuel, she'd have to make the idiot move. Otherwise, one of the two cars was sure to get hit, what with Hottie having left his right at the pump, too.

Maybe Baldy just wants to stretch his legs or put air in his tires, she prayed.

No such luck. The idiot was on his way into the café.

Worse yet, he walked right over to Hottie and sat down across the booth from him.

They nodded, but didn't say a word to each other. Miffed, she cut a slice of the pie and poured the coffee. Before walking over to them, she slipped a menu under her arm.

The dishes clattered as she laid the plate and mug in front of Hottie. She practically slung the menu at Baldy. But before she could flounce away, Hottie grabbed her by the wrist. "He'll have what I'm having," he said with a chuckle.

She replied tartly, "Sure, he will."

She had no doubt he was watching her as she sauntered off. Suddenly she wondered, did I just promise to give Baldy a quickie too? No...Hell no! Oh sure, she'd been the sweetmeat in a middle of a manwich on a few occasions. But this time she wanted her focus to be on no one but Hottie.

She'd make sure he saw it that way, too, if push came to shove. She certainly knew what to push, and where to shove it.

The men's voices were too low for her to hear what they were saying, not that Baldy said much of anything. It seemed that Hottie did all the talking. Baldy just shook his head and frowned. When he spoke at all, the words came out in an unintelligible growl.

When she placed Baldy's food in front of him, she noticed he had a ring on his pinky finger. It was gold, with a black shiny crest. Also outlined in gold was the number, "13." Usually if someone was wearing something unique, she'd coo out a comment in the hope that they'd leave a bigger tip. Instead, she kept her mouth shut. The look in Baldy's eyes sent a chill up her spine.

She was relieved when, a moment later, he got up and walked out the door. By the time he pulled out of the parking lot, Hottie had also risen. He didn't look too happy —until he realized she was walking his way. Then the devilish smile was back. "What do I owe you?"

She shrugged. "For two coffees and pies, it's seven-fifty."

He opened his wallet and pulled out another twenty. He folded it and placed it in the deep crest between her breasts. "Keep the change."

Before he could remove his hand, she pressed it against her breast.

He didn't pull away.

They were interrupted by a dull buzz coming from his cell phone.

He pulled it out of his pocket and stared down at it, but he didn't answer it.

When he laid it down on the tabletop, she knew he didn't care who was on the other end of that line.

That made two of them.

She eased herself onto the table. Then she grabbed ahold of his belt buckle and pulled him toward her. His response was to lift her skirt and hook her thong with his index finger. Slowly, he pulled it down her thigh—

But they froze when they heard a cacophony of horns. In unison, they looked up to see a trio of eighteen-wheelers circling the gas pumps.

"Aw, hell," Hottie muttered as he ran out the door.

Seeing him, one of the truckers rolled down his window

and hollered, "Yo, buddy, you're blocking the diesel pumps! Better move that ballet slipper before it gets sideswiped."

Two of the other truckers were already parked and making their way into the café. As Hottie brushed by them, one poked the other in the rib and snickered.

Hottie stopped in his tracks. He turned around to face the man. He stood there for a moment, still and silent.

Then he punched the trucker in his throat.

While his buddy lay gasping on the hot asphalt, the other trucker raised his hands as a sign of surrender.

Hottie stared at the trucker for what seemed like an eternity. The fear in the man's eyes sent a shiver down Jolene's spine.

Realizing that the trucker wasn't going to give him any trouble, Hottie looked back at Jolene, grinned wickedly, then strolled to his car.

She watched as the Carrera backed out of the lot and peeled off.

Then she noticed Hottie's cell had fallen onto the booth's cushioned seat.

Hmmm. Maybe Beth was right, and he really was an actor—in martial arts movies or something. She didn't see enough of them to know for sure.

She was sorely tempted to open the cell phone's directory and scroll through the contact information. The only thing that stopped her was the hope that he'd come back when he realized he'd left it, and she'd hate it if he caught her snooping.

That hope stayed with her the rest of the night.

At daybreak when, as she served the four-day-old pie to two deputies from the Joshua Tree Sheriff's Department along with another coffee refill, one of them mentioned something about a Porsche that "had to have been doing close to ninety miles an hour before it rolled and burst into flames."

Jolene felt the blood rush from her face. "Was it a black Carrera?"

Seeing the look of horror on her face, he nodded solemnly and added, "By the time the fire truck got there, it was an inferno. Burned so hot, it incinerated the body. Nothing was left but ashes."

She was so stunned that she dropped the coffee pot as she ran to the ladies' room to throw up.

By the time she remembered she had Hottie's phone, the patrolmen had cleared out. She didn't feel guilty holding onto it.

Later at home, when she opened it, she was disappointed to find it locked with a security code. Now she'd have to wait to see if *People* or *Us Weekly* mentioned the accident. Should it turn out he was someone after all, at least she'd always have it, as a memento.

Hell, it might be valuable, even more so now that he was dead. If she'd learned anything on the night shift, it was that sometimes patience paid off.

5

The Spy Who Came in from the Cold

Every now and then, a spy vanishes in an attempt to escape the web of deceit in which he is forever tangled.

If he never resurfaces, it's due to one of four possible reasons:

1. *He is truly off the digital, social, and communal grid, and therefore has left no trace of his existence;*
2. *He has successfully changed his identity, which means he's successfully taken on a new one, and most certainly a new face as well;*
3. *He has enough dirt on his employers for them to leave him alone; or*
4. *Bang, bang, he's dead, thanks to the employer who sends in the clean-up crew, or an old enemy with an ax to grind—on the gone guy's neck.*

Should the missing agent resurface eventually, it's only because (a) he's not dead; and (b) he wants to be found.

Be duly warned: he, too, may have a few axes to grind, so watch your back...and your neck.

JACK'S HEADACHE WAS A CLEAR INDICATION THAT HE'D GONE TO bed drunk.

Again.

If he needed further proof, all he had to do was look at the empty Scotch bottle rolling back and forth on the floor of the one-hundred-year-old antique mahogany cabin cruiser he now called home.

He'd won the cabin cruiser from a down-on-his-luck Irish seaman, thanks to a backdoor straight in a Texas Hold'em game at Charly's, the only casino on the French Riviera that was still willing to let him play, especially after the unfortunate incident at Le Baoli that included a scuffle with the lobby boy of the Hotel Cannes de Croissette, and a chimpanzee he'd emancipated from *Le Parc Zoologique de Frejus*.

The boat came with its own crew: three blondes who claimed to be dancers from the Monte Carlo Ballet who thought the chimp was—how did they put it? Oh yes, *"être un bourreau de coeurs"*—a ladykiller.

"That makes two of us," Jack muttered under his breath.

The waves slapping against the boat were gentle enough now. But last night they were rougher. Every so often the bottle slammed into an empty tin basin on the far side of the galley. Whenever this happened, Jack's ears interpreted it as the start of Armageddon. He'd slide out of the bed, his Sig cocked and pointed in the direction of the perceived danger.

Depending on their own state of mind or ability to hold their liquor, either the women would squeal in fear, or moan through their hangover headache, or hiccup obliviously.

The gun had never rattled the chimp. In fact, Monsieur Muggles clapped heartily whenever Jack fired it, but the damn thing also snickered whenever he missed his target, which was much too often these days, what with the amount of Scotch he'd been consuming.

Monsieur Muggles had been great company. Jack was sorry it had finally run off. Bored, Jack presumed.

On the other hand, the blondes, now sprawled out naked and asleep on his bed, were there to stay.

As bored as he was with them, perhaps he should have followed Monsieur Muggles' lead and gotten the hell out of there.

They were nothing like his ex.

He wondered if he'd ever get over her.

Perhaps if he quit drinking, he'd have a chance to find her.

He'd have to quit the blondes, too.

It was a trade he'd willingly make.

As if reading his mind, the man standing on the other side of the bed asked, "Be honest. Can you tell them apart?"

For once, Jack didn't reach for his gun. In fact, he didn't even need to turn around because he recognized the voice as Ryan Clancy's, his boss and the director of Acme Industries.

Jack sighed. He was loath to admit he couldn't tell one woman from another, even when sober. They insisted they weren't sisters, but each was generously breasted and long-legged, not to mention doe-eyed and snub-nosed. Most times, they talked in unison.

At least they shut up during sex.

He shrugged. "Nah, but I've got a system. Here, I'll show you."

He threw back the sheet, exposing the naked bodies of the women. The one closest to him was on her side, in the fetal position. He nudged her so that she flopped over onto her belly, revealing her backside. At the base of her spine was a tattoo with the word FAUNA. Above it was the image of one of the plump fairies from Disney's *Sleeping Beauty* cartoon.

He pointed to the woman next to her, who was already sleeping ass-side up. She too was branded, only her tramp stamp stated FLORA, and was also accompanied by another of the cartoon's fairies.

Ryan's brows rose. He tilted his head toward the one woman who was still facing them. She snored gently as she cuddled her pillow to her breasts. "Let me guess. This one is labeled 'Merriweather.'"

"You'll have to take my word for it—that is unless you'd like to see for yourself."

"No need to disturb her. Besides, the view from this angle is just fine." Ryan stared down at the woman's plump breasts. "Considering the length of the name, she's quite a trooper."

"In more ways than one." Jack scooped a shirt off the floor and put it on, but left it unbuttoned over his jeans. "How did you find me, anyway?"

"We got a call from French Intelligence. Something about a monkey—and a maître d'."

"It was a chimpanzee—and a lobby boy."

"Tomato, to-*mah*-toe." Ryan shrugged. "Apparently when

you're in your cups, you have a very bad habit of getting into fights. Stop me if I'm wrong, but if it weren't for your Acme get-out-of-jail free card, by now you'd have had the opportunity to see the inside of every hoosegow along the French Rivera. So yeah, say goodbye to your playmates. The vacation is over."

"It's not a vacation. I'm in mourning."

"From the looks of things, you're well on the road to recovery."'

"Looks are deceiving." The blondes beside him were certainly proof of that. "Believe me, you really don't want me anywhere near Acme." He took a deep breath. Okay, he thought, let the chips fall where they may. "Ryan, I lost the microdot with the code to Acme's Agents and Assets Directory."

That certainly got Ryan's attention.

He didn't turn toward Jack when he asked calmly, "Did your ex take it with her?"

Jack shook his head. "I...I don't know. But I don't think so. I never mentioned it to her, and it wasn't among our mutual belongings. I truly thought I'd hid it well." He shrugged. "If you're asking me if the timing is coincidental, then yes, I'm sorry to say."

Jack winced as Ryan's head turned in Jack's direction. The fact that the rest of his body didn't follow was a good sign. After what Ryan just heard, Jack would not have been surprised to see Ryan pull his Sig from the holster hidden beneath his jacket and drill him right between the eyes.

Hell, it's what I deserve, he thought.

"The reason I ask—the reason I thought it was worth finding you—is that the family alias Acme assigned to her popped up on the flight manifest for a plane that went down four days ago."

Seeing the shocked expression on Jack's face, he continued, "It was an Air India private charter, from Johannesburg to Caracas, soon after takeoff around two hundred miles from shore." After letting the news sink in, he added, "Jack, is there any reason she may have been in South Africa, or for that matter, headed to Venezuela?"

"My best guess is that she was running as far away from me as possible." His voice cracked with pain. "If you remember, she had her reasons to hate what we do for a living." His head bowed under the weight of his memories of his wife. They'd had too many fights about it.

He tried to shake off his anguish. "When will we know for sure if it's her, or some other poor soul with that name?"

"The airline has asked NTSB to help in the investigation, but the water is pretty deep there. Should they recover the black box, it's doubtful they'll be pulling up bodies as well." Ryan sighed. "I'll say prayers that it's an anomaly. However, if she was on the plane—Jack, you know you have my deepest condolences. As for whether your wife somehow grabbed Acme's Agent and Asset Directory when she headed out the door, there is a way in which we can find out if it was compromised."

"What?" Jack stuttered. "But...how?"

"Arnie coded all agents' and administrators' microdots with a specific verifier. Besides tracking which agent's code has been entered and where in the world the access is taking place, it verifies the agent's personal GPS coordinates. Even if there's a match—say, the agent is there, but is accessing the files under duress—there's a trick identifier."

Jack had to ask, "Has anyone tried to sign in as me?"

"No, which makes me believe that perhaps the microdot was misplaced accidentally." Ryan shrugged. "I'm glad you came clean about the loss before we found out the hard way. Based on what you've just told me, the only thing saving your ass from a one-way ticket to Gitmo is that none of our agents or assets have been exterminated, as of yet—which tells me it may be hiding in plain sight." Ryan nodded toward the door. "Jack, I'm giving you a chance to redeem yourself, if you'll take it."

Jack's lips curled into a grimace. "You mean my fuck-ups haven't made me expendable?"

Ryan laughed. "Not yet, anyway. If you head up this investigation, you might actually be Acme's salvation."

"What will I be investigating?"

Ryan paused, then muttered, "Carl Stone's death."

Carl...

Was dead?

"It was a Quorum hit."

Oh, hell, Jack thought.

He had no one to blame but himself. "You're sure of it?" He knew his voice was shaking.

"I wouldn't be here if I wasn't." Ryan's statement was anchored with a weariness Jack had never heard before.

"Ryan, Tatyana was there. She came with the producer, Ross Tanner, and some short, bald guy who wore glasses and a pinky ring. When they were escaping, I shot Ross. But I couldn't stop them from getting away."

"Interesting. We've suspected for some time that Ross was a Quorum asset."

"Good then. At least I got one of Carl's killers." Jack tried to smile about it.

Ryan winced. "We're still waiting for confirmation on that. No one matching his description was found in the canal, or in a Venice morgue. But at the same time, Ross Tanner hasn't showed up on any flight manifests out of Venice, or on any Los Angeles flights. And oddly enough, his wife has disappeared as well. They had no children. Recently, his film projects were put on hold while the production company's assets were sold, along with his real estate holdings."

Jack frowned. "But Carl gave you the thumb drive, didn't he?"

"No. He called to say he was on his way into Acme head-quarters to drop it off when his wife, Donna went into labor. He never made it. He also had something else in his posses-sion that they desperately wanted. At least, that's what we gather from the chatter we're hearing online. It's the reason he was in Paris in the first place."

For a moment, Jack heard nothing at all: not the gulls shrieking, or the waves lapping the dock pilings. Not even the gentle snores of Flora, Fauna, and Merriweather.

Nothing, except the bottle as it skittered across the floor.

As it rolled past, he stopped it with his foot, then reached down and picked it up.

By holding the bottle upright, he could tell there were at least a few sips left.

Yes, he was tempted to take a swig.

Instead, he tossed it out the galley porthole.

It landed in the sea with a loud splash.

Ryan smiled. "Welcome back."

6

Dossier

A dossier is a collection or file of documents on the same subject, especially a complete file containing detailed information about a person or topic. A government's intelligence agencies will create a dossier on (a) agency personnel, (b) persons of interest, and (c) known threats to the country in question.

Should such a file be collated on your behalf, you can be sure it would contain (a) every pertinent recorded document that has ever been filed on you, (b) comments from everyone who has had an opinion about you, and (c) a full and comprehensive compendium of your dirty little secrets.

There is a natural desire to take a peek inside your own dossier. If given the chance, should you take it? Just remember: sticks and stones may break your bones, but words—not to mention pictures and certified documents—may be the end of life as you know it.

～

"SEE HERE, THE WAY WE FIGURE IT, YOUR BUDDY THE DECEASED was revving that baby at full tilt boogie—say, a hundred and a quarter—before he lost control." The Yucca County Sheriff's deputy spat out a bit of the straw he'd been chewing. "Maybe he was trying to avoid a jackrabbit or something. Anyhoo, our guess is that the car flipped a bazillion times, then burst into flames."

The first step in Jack's investigation was to see the scene of Carl's demise. Abu Nagashahi, another Acme operative who was also an explosives expert, had been assigned to go with him.

Both stared at the crater in the middle of the road, where Carl Stone's Porsche Carrera hadn't just exploded—

It had *disintegrated*.

At least, that was the way some trucker described it to the deputy who'd been sent to investigate the crash scene. The accident happened right on Highway 62—or what the locals called Twentynine Palms Highway. The trucker had been following behind the Carrera, albeit thirty miles-per-hour slower, which put him a good ten minutes behind. The only reason he'd been able to keep the Carrera in his sights was that this stretch of blacktop is pencil straight. But after the road hooked south—just west of Steeg Road above Sand Pit Ranch road—he lost sight of the sports car, until he rounded the corner himself.

By then, what was left of the car was a massive fireball leaping skyward.

"You said you think he skidded to avoid a turtle or something?" Abu scratched his head. "I see the eighteen-wheeler's skid marks, but none from the Carrera, which means he didn't slow down, let alone swerve off the road."

The deputy gave Abu a blank stare.

Abu shrugged then mouthed the word *bomb* to Jack.

The deputy bristled. "What did you say, smartass?" He turned to Jack. "Did he just speak Arabic?"

Jack shook his head. "Bomb is an English word. As in, VBIED, or Vehicle Borne Improvised Explosive Device. You've heard of C4, right? Plastic explosives?"

The deputy chewed down his blade of straw another couple of inches as he thought that one through. "Well whattaya know! And all this time we thought it was a case of spontaneous combustion."

Jack dropped his head and sighed loudly. "That's a myth."

"Oh, I beg to differ, sir. I saw a documentary about it, on the SciFi Channel, so it's most certainly true."

Jack's silence spoke volumes on what he thought about the deputy's television viewing habits.

The deputy shrugged. "Okay, let's say you're right. What makes you think it was some sort of bomb?"

Abu shrugged. "The size of the crater, for starters. And the trucker mentioned a fireball shooting skyward, right? Then there's the fact that the car and everything was blown up, and sadly, Carl Stone along with it. Even if we find the charred chassis, the airtight design of the Carrera assures that any DNA would be incinerated beyond analysis."

"Ha. Maybe you're right. You know, I hear Al Qaeda stole a whole bunch of missiles and launchers and shit from Saddam's stash, when Iran fell."

"Iraq," Jack muttered.

The deputy tilted his hat far back on the crown of head. "Beg pardon?"

"Saddam Hussein ruled Iraq, not Iran."

The sheriff guffawed. "Shee-it! What difference does it make? They're all a bunch of towelheads, ain't they?" He turned to Abu. "Of course I mean no disrespect."

"No, of course not," Abu muttered under his breath. He took out a laser distance measurer and walked over to the hole.

While he went about the business of measuring it, Jack turned to the deputy. "So, are you telling me that there are Al Qaeda terrorists out here in the middle of this desert?"

The deputy chewed his cud on that one for a good minute or two. Finally he said, "It's a big fucking desert. Isn't that where they like to, you know, run their jihadist camps? Hell, I hear they cross the border all the time, coming in with the wetbacks." He gave Abu a sideways glance.

Abu dead-eyed right back at him. "I'm *Sikh*."

"Then don't sneeze on me. I can't afford to be laid up with germs, especially ones from a foreigner." The sheriff took a tissue from his pocket and covered his mouth with it. "Them Al Qaeda boys have stolen enough of them heat-seeking missiles and launchers from Egypt to blow up every truck that comes barreling down this road for a month. Maybe they were testing a launcher on your buddy's sports car."

Jack's sunglasses were tinted enough that the deputy couldn't see his eyes grow big with disbelief over the man's stupidity.

"The crater is twenty-three feet, seven inches at its widest point," Abu shouted back at them. "And six feet-four inches deep, in the center. Fifty, maybe sixty pounds of plastic explosives could make that size dent. The bomb wasn't set with a timer, since whoever did it wanted Carl in the car when it went off. It might have been set off by remote control, but since the trucker said no one else was on the road but the two of them, we can rule that out. Instead, it was rigged to go off at a speed exceeding ninety-five miles-per-hour." Abu shook his head in awe. "Considering how low the chassis rides, it's lucky he wasn't in a more populated area when it blew."

"I see he's a bomb expert, eh? Figures." By now, the grass straw between the deputy's thin lips was a mere nub.

"Look, Deputy, was there anything the trucker said that might provide additional information? For example, did another car pass him before he came up on the crater?"

"Well, yeah, he did say something I thought strange at the time. But now...well, I can see how it makes sense." Deputy Dumbass looked down at the steaming blacktop, as if in a trance. Then he leaned in toward Jack and whispered, "Aliens."

Jack shook his head, annoyed. "The US Government spent thirteen million dollars last year securing the borders. Considering it's two and a half hours from the Mexican border, and we're out here in the middle of nowhere, what would illegal aliens have to do with anything?"

The deputy shook his head, amused. "Right now I ain't talking about the wetback kind. I meant the kind...well, you know! *Up there*." He pointed overhead.

Jack couldn't believe his ears. Still, he managed to keep a straight face when he asked, "So, this trucker thinks the car was beamed up into an alien space ship?"

The deputy nodded his head. "Yep, exactly! That would explain a lot, dontcha think?"

"Yeah. Right." *Wrong.* Jack stroked his chin. This kept his trigger finger busy. Otherwise, he'd be tempted to put Deputy Dumbass out of his misery. "Of course, that doesn't explain why Carl's car is right over there."

He pointed to the parched desert floor on their left. About a quarter of a mile away, the charred body of the vehicle could be spotted. Abu had already looked it over. Shaking his head, he explained, "The velocity of the fall slammed it into the ground, crushing everything inside. Anybody inside would have been pulverized."

While the sheriff watched, Jack and Abu circled the area between the crater and the car, in the hope of finding Carl's body, but no luck.

"Even if there was something left of him—say, a limb—it could have been carried off by a coyote, since the sheriff's department's search didn't take place until daylight," Abu muttered to Jack.

"I myself lean toward the theory that a meteor fell out of the sky," the deputy insisted. "Fate works in mysterious ways, my friends. One moment, a man's eating a piece of pie at a shit-hole truck stop, the next moment he's barreling down the road, only to be blown sky-high—"

"Wait!" Jack stared at the officer. "Did you say Carl stopped somewhere?"

"Didn't I mention that before?...No? Been forgetful lately, probably this damn heat. I need to start drinking more of that Ginko Bonobo stuff, and less Jack Daniels. As I remember, your friend gassed up at the Hot Wheels All-Nite Truck Stop. Jolene waited on him. I know this because when she heard what happened to him, she darn near went to pieces.

You'd think he'd asked her to marry him and not just banged her on the counter."

Jack's brow went up an inch. "Is that what she said, that he screwed her?"

"She didn't have to say anything. Three truckers pulled up while they were getting it on. Hey, it's no reflection on your buddy, believe me. That gal's got quite a reputation. She's known as the trucker's dream of Highway 62."

This time when Deputy Dumbass spit, he sprayed some of it on Jack's shoes.

Jack suppressed his urge to frown, let alone yank the deputy by his necktie down on his knees and order him to wipe the spittle off his shoes.

Instead, he murmured, "Your insights have been invaluable, Deputy. Thanks for your time."

"You say you're a friend of poor dearly departed Hottie?" If Jolene had any interest in the handsome stranger standing in front of her—and hell yeah, she did—it just increased fourfold.

Jack's mouth turned up at the edges. "Is that what you called him, 'Hottie'?"

"Not to his face, *per se*. It wasn't as if we were formerly introduced or anything. But something tells me I could have called him anything and he wouldn't have minded." Jolene batted her lashes. "I'm just here to serve, if you catch my drift."

To make sure he did, Jolene leaned over the counter as far

as she could, just in case for some silly reason he hadn't noticed her breasts—difficult to imagine, considering they were practically falling out of her too tight and too-low-cut uniform.

Still, New Hottie's eyes never left hers—something she found confusing at first, to say the least. Soon, though, she felt it, like a Vulcan mind meld or something. She'd never considered Mr. Spock to be the sexiest of the *Star Trek* characters. She was more of a Captain Kirk girl, herself. To her mind, Dr. Bones came in a close second, with Scotty bringing up the rear, if only because she couldn't see herself with a man who yelled, "I'm giving it all I've got" all the time.

With Jolene, you didn't promise.

You delivered.

No doubt, New Hottie never let a girl down.

She'd be willing to find out first-hand.

"So, tell me, Miss Caruthers—that is Jolene." He leaned in, too, and smiled. "Did Hottie—I mean, Mr. Stone mention where he was headed?"

She pursed her lips. At least, she thought she was pursing them. She had a Collagen injection the day before, so for all she knew she might have been gulping like a guppy. She just hoped that her mouth looked inviting. Hell, it better. Her lips were so inflated that it took half her lip-gloss to look decent—a new shade called Inner Labia, whatever that meant. All she knew was that it was pink, shiny, and tasted like strawberries. If she played her cards right, he'd be leaning in for a taste of it, too. "He didn't exactly say, no. I thought he was headed back to LA because he was dressed so nice and all. But they said the crash happened east of here, beyond Steeg." If she could rustle up a few crocodile tears, she wondered if he'd try to comfort her. If he cuddled her to his chest, it would be worth smearing her supposedly waterproof eyeliner.

"So, in other words, the only thing he did was pay for a tank of gas?" New Hottie frowned.

Jolene had too much pride to let a man walk away disappointed, inside or outside of a restroom stall. "No, I wouldn't say that! I mean…he also bought two pieces of pie and two coffees."

Hearing that, New Hottie seemed interested again. "So, you sat down to join him."

"No, not me, silly! Some short, bald dude."

Jack put his hand over hers. "Anything else you can remember about him?"

That was all the encouragement she needed to at least pretend to remember something. She tried to furrow her brow, but recent Botox injections made that an impossible feat. She sighed, frustrated. "Your pal had just paid for his gas when Baldy drove up—not in any sports car or nothing, just some car your granny would drive, only newer."

Jack nodded encouragingly. "What else, Jolene. Please think hard, because it's important."

"Oh…well, he was in his fifties. He certainly wasn't dressed as nice as Hottie. By that I mean, no suit or nothing. Sports jacket and khakis, like any other middle-aged man. And he had glasses, too. Not sunglasses, but round ones, like Harry Potter. I remember because he was dripping with sweat, and the lenses fogged over when he walked in here."

The way Jack jotted down what she said in his little pad made her feel important, for once in her life. There was something else about the man that was unique. What was it again? Oh yeah—

"And he was wearing this pinky ring."

Jack quit writing and looked up at her. "Really? Can you describe it?"

"Sure! It was platinum, but it had a big black flat area, where a stone would go. I guess the guy couldn't afford one. Instead, it had some writing on it...a number."

He reached out for her hand. "What number?"

"It was thirteen."

~

BINGO, JACK THOUGHT.

Jolene's Baldy has to be the same man who left Leonid's party with Tatyana and Ross. Well, this certainly verifies Ryan's suspicions that the Quorum carried out the hit on Carl.

"Jolene, you didn't happen to overhear any of their conversation, did you?" He patted her hand encouragingly.

"Not exactly. But I do know that Hottie—I mean, Carl—wasn't too happy with whatever Baldy had to say because Carl didn't say much in return, and he frowned the whole time."

Maybe while Pinky Ring was distracting Carl, someone was rigging Carl's car with explosives, Jack thought. "Did they park side by side?"

"No. Carl, the bad boy, left his car at the pump. See that big ol' 'No Parking' sign? Baldy pulled in over there. Of course, you can't expect foreigners to know how to read English, I suppose."

"How did you know he was a foreigner?"

"He spoke with an accent."

"Was it a German one?'

She shrugged. "Could have been. I'm only an expert on the romance languages. *Comprende, amigo?*"

By the way she entwined her fingers in his, Jack could tell she was getting bored from talking about something other than herself. Too bad for her. Aside from the fact that she wasn't his type, he needed to get back to Los Angeles as soon as possible and fill Ryan in on these developments.

He locked eyes with her once more as he handed her a card that identified him as Jack Craig, Vice President of Prime 1 Bank. "Here's my private number. If you think of anything else, don't hesitate to call."

THE LOOK IN HIS EYE—OF TRUE APPRECIATION, AS IF WHAT SHE told him held the key to secrets of the universe—gave her something she never had before:

An overwhelming degree of self-respect.

Hell, this is better than sex, she thought.

Still on a high from it, right then and there, she made a brash decision. She reached under the counter where she had hidden Carl Stone's cell phone behind a box of plastic knives and handed it to Jack.

"This belonged to your friend. He left it here that night. He turned it off when we..." Suddenly shy, she hesitated. "I mean, when some truckers came in, bitching because he'd left his car at one of the pumps. I know someone was trying real hard to reach him."

To thank her, he shook her hand firmly.

Then he kissed her on the forehead.

By the time he'd driven off, Jolene had already made the decision to quit the truck stop. There had to be something better in life than being the Trucker's Dream along Highway 62.

Maybe she'd follow her dream—live in Las Vegas.

Last time she was there, they were looking for bar maids in her favorite hotel, New York New York. Slinging drinks there had to earn her better tips than delivering a side of fries and a burger in this dump.

Not to mention that the town was filled with hotties.

Jolene didn't need a dead man's cell phone. She needed a live guy's love.

She didn't wait for her shift to end. She rolled out the door without once looking back.

7

Collection

A thorough investigation requires the collection of intelligence from numerous sources.

If these sources involve technical data, it falls into one of these categories: signals intelligence (SIGNINT); measurement and signature intelligence (MASINT); open-source intelligence (OSINT), and imagery intelligence (IMINT).

If the intelligence gathered comes from an individual based on what they saw, overheard, actually experienced, actively engaged in or initiated, or were witnessed doing, it's known as human intelligence (HUMINT).

Whereas technical intel is quantitative, HUMINT is subject to perception, memory, and supposition. That said, when it comes to HUMINT, remember this:

Truth is in the eye of the collector!

"Okay, let's review what we've got so far, from the

beginning," Ryan said to Jack and Arnie, the tech op assigned to the investigation.

The three men were sprawled out around one of the conference tables in Acme headquarters. Outside, the sky was a dry bright blue. It was late afternoon, and already cars were backed up on the Ventura Freeway, the roadway just beyond the greenbelt outside the room's floor-to-ceiling windows.

"Let's look at the big picture. A man leaves his wife at a Los Angeles area hospital as she goes into labor on the excuse that he forgot her maternity bag, but never shows back up," Ryan continued. "Several hours later, it's confirmed that his car blew up near the Arizona border."

"If the trucker following behind him hadn't memorized the license plate when Carl passed him, would we have even known it was his car, or what direction he was headed?" Jack wondered out loud.

"Yeah, sure," Arnie assured him. "I could have traced him via his car's GPS record."

Jack shook his head. "Carl was too smart for that. He would have dismantled the GPS the moment he realized he was being followed, or tracked."

Ryan nodded. "That's where this all started, remember? Carl found the GPS tracker, which had been planted on his car. The fact that he put it in Donna's maternity bag was one way to buy time. The Quorum would assume he'd spent the night traipsing the floor, like any other anxious, expectant father. It would also tip us off to the realization that he was on the run."

"There's another way I could have traced him, but it would have taken a heck of a lot of time to do it." Arnie hesitated. "I could have pulled up the hospital's security web cam feeds from the time he left the hospital to retrieve the bag, then followed him via the street and highway feeds to the new house they'd just moved into, back to the hospital, and beyond."

"Which means, the Quorum could have also done that," Jack pointed out.

"Which brings us to the Hot Wheels Truck Stop," Jack added. "Arnie, what did you pull from the café's video cams?"

"It has two of them," Arnie explained. "One, which is fixed in place, is on the canopy over the pumps. The other scans the truck parking lot. Carl drove up in the evening, so there's a lot of shadow, and their equipment has a lousy digital feed to begin with, but you can still make him out at the pump. From the looks of things, at first he reached for his credit card, but then he decided to pay cash for his gasoline purchase."

Ryan nodded. "That makes sense. If he felt someone was following him, that would make it harder to trace his whereabouts."

"The other man she mentioned parked off to one side. I was able to isolate one frame for a photo, but like I said, the camera is crap, and even blown up, the shot is fuzzy." Arnie pointed to a picture on the table.

Jack picked it up for a closer look. "It's not a great shot, but that's Pinky Ring alright."

"It was a lucky break that the waitress gave Carl's cell phone to Jack," Arnie continued. "But unfortunately, by the time we realized he was missing, the battery was dead. I couldn't have traced his GPS coordinates in any event, since his cell is tied to Acme's GPS jammer and our secure satellite. It's why the Quorum put a tracker on his car in the first place."

"At least Acme now knows the answer as to why his cell phone's last known GPS coordinates don't coincide with the location of the bombsite," Jack added. "What else can Carl's phone tell us, Arnie?"

"Not much. There are three sets of fingerprints on it," Arnie admitted. "They belong to Carl, his wife Donna, and the waitress, Jolene."

"Have you been able to trace any of the calls that were made to it before the battery died?" Ryan asked.

"You mean, other than ones from his wife?" Arnie shook his head. "Like most terrorist organizations—and for that matter, black-ops groups like Acme—the cell phones of Quorum operatives have some sort of GPS jammer."

"How about his cell's contact directory?" Ryan asked.

"Empty," Arnie declared.

"Was there a reason for his wife to field his calls, or scan his directory?" Jack asked. He jotted down this thought, with a question mark.

"If he left it on the nightstand by the bed, there's always a chance she picked it up to move it, or to hand it to him," Ryan reasoned. He paused then added, "In any event, I don't want you questioning her."

Jack looked up sharply. "Why not? In the months leading up to Carl going on the run, she may have noticed some odd behavioral pattern that would be of use to the investigation."

Ryan shook his head firmly. "Donna knew nothing of his life as an assassin. And besides the fact that she's shaken to the core over his death, the classified aspect of this investigation means we have to keep her in the dark about our findings."

"Wow, talk about clueless," Jack murmured.

Ryan shrugged. "Not necessarily. She didn't come out and say so, but when I came clean with Carl's real position at Acme, I could tell she knew something was up, if not exactly what. Carl was certainly adept at keeping her in the dark. It may also have been why he wanted to move his family to a gated community—Hilldale, in Orange County."

Arnie typed something into his iPad. Up came a live 3D map. He let loose with a low whistle. "Talk about McMansionLand! Hilldale has the typical bells and whistles you find in these über-environs—great schools, excellent shopping, top notch restaurants for the parental units, tricked out parks for the kiddies, not to mention around-the-clock security. The whole place is walled up, like a fortress." He swiped the screen a few times until he found what he was looking for. "Ah, here we go—the architect's floor plan of the Stone's casa grande." He zoomed in, then let loose with a low whistle. "Wow! Carl put in a customized security system, and a state-of-the-art panic room, too. Looks like he was preparing for Armageddon."

"You're starting to sound like an infomercial," Jack muttered. He turned to Ryan. "Did Mrs. Stone give you any idea where he may have hidden the intel in his possession?"

Ryan shook his head. "We were hoping he put it in the bag he dropped off at the hospital for her, but it wasn't there."

"Heck, I even pulled apart the baby's teddy bear, to make sure he hadn't slipped it into the stuffing," Arnie added.

"Donna noticed your handiwork and she wasn't too

happy about it." Ryan frowned. "When she got home from the hospital, she realized that someone had gone through their personal possessions as well. I didn't admit it to her, but I'd sent Abu over there. He came up empty-handed. Ironically, he feels someone beat him to the punch."

"Maybe the Quorum found the intel after all," Jack said. Frustrated, he pounded his fist on the table.

"We'll know for sure if Carl's family is left alone from here on out," Ryan reasoned. "However, some things were missing: according to Donna, every picture of Carl was gone."

"He could have done that himself," Arnie declared. "Especially if his game plan was to go off the grid."

"Maybe he took the intel with him as a bargaining chip." Jack hated to throw that supposition out there, but considering he was a marked man with a wife and kids, he could see why Carl would do so.

Ryan turned toward Jack, "If so, in all likelihood the intel was blown to smithereens along with him."

"She also mentioned there was nothing out of the ordinary in his behavior before the night he left. I spoke as candidly as I could with her in order to assess what she knew about his undercover assignment with the Quorum. Needless to say, she knew nothing about his true position with us."

"I'll bet it was a shock," Jack muttered. He'd witnessed Carl's charm when in the presence of a pretty woman. Then he remembered Jolene. Even when he wasn't present, Carl left a lasting impression.

Ryan threw up his hands in frustration. "We're coming up dry."

"In that case, let me interview the Widow Stone." Jack leaned in to make his point.

"Are you kidding?" Ryan exclaimed. "No way. Her husband just died, she just found out her husband lied to her, she just had a baby, and she's now facing the reality of raising three kids by herself. She's stunned, upset, and depressed. The way she feels about Acme right now, she'll throw you out on your ass—especially if you give her the impression you think she was naïve about Carl."

"Let me guess," Jack said, "She's a dumb blonde." Carl's type, from what he'd seen.

"In fact, she's a brunette. And sharp as a tack. But hell, if the Quorum comes calling, she and her kids are sitting ducks —" Ryan's tapping fingers suddenly stopped. "I've got an idea. The community is fairly new. Abu noticed that there were still a lot of empty houses on the block. In fact, the one directly across the street had a for rent sign in the yard. I'll lease it immediately. That should make surveillance much easier on you."

Arnie gave Ryan a thumbs up. "Great! Anything to get me off my mom's couch!" He turned to Jack. "We can be roomies."

Jack winced. "Wow. Great." He turned to Ryan. "I presume you'll want us to do a more thorough sweep of the Stone residence, when it's convenient. With three kids, I suppose she has cause to leave the house, if only to go grocery shopping and take the older ones to and from school."

"With three children, I'm sure she does a hell of a lot more than just that," Ryan muttered. "Yeah, okay. Just find what Carl left behind—and Jack, do it fast. When you do, we'll leak it so that the Quorum has no reason to hang around." Ryan shifted uneasily in his seat. "And don't get caught! The last thing she needs is to think that Acme is spying on her. If so, all the trust I'm trying to build with her will go right out the window."

"No problem. She won't even know I'm there." Jack turned to Arnie. "First things first—we'll need to plant a few eyes and ears in her place."

"Piece of cake," Arnie assured him.

Ryan snorted.

Jack raised a brow. "What's so funny?"

"Jack Craig of all places—in suburbia." Ryan shook his head. "Fair warning—even tricked out, it's not the home-and-hearth country club utopia it seems. Don't trust anyone."

8

Black Bag Job

When the mission is to break into a home or office, it's called a black bag job.

Unlike a con job, which is when a grifter cheats you out of money.

Or a screw job, when someone lets you down or even worse, breaks your heart.

Or a blowjob when someone...never mind.

No matter what kind of "job," the target feels violated.

And yes, someday, somehow, all of us are targets.

"That must be her." Arnie nodded toward the front door of the house across the street.

With lightning speed, Jack, who had been busy unpacking some of their surveillance gear, grabbed a pair of binoculars and ducked below the large bowed window just in time to see a woman emerging from the Stone residence—240 Hilldale Drive.

She was nothing like he'd imagined. She was just...normal.

She was of medium height—from where she stood in the threshold of the door, he estimated she was five feet and six inches, maybe five-seven. And she was slender and small-boned, with none of the baby fat that you see on most women who have just delivered a child.

Then again, most women don't lose their husbands on the very same night.

Donna Stone's hair, straight and brown, fell just below her shoulders. Her face was pretty enough—her nose turned up slightly at the end, her cheekbones were high, all the more emphasized by her heart-shaped face and her small cupid-bow mouth.

Just at that moment, she turned her face directly to him—

And smiled.

Seeing it, straight on, he realized why Carl had fallen in love with her.

It must have been that look in her wide, deep-set blue eyes. Despite the sadness he saw in them, there was also steely determination.

It would be so easy to fall in love with Donna Stone.

Jack shook the thought out of his mind.

He watched as Donna turned her head back into the house, making a sweeping motion with her hands. Suddenly two small children appeared at her side. An older woman came out, too. She was holding an infant in a handheld carrier.

"That's Phyllis Lindholm, Donna's aunt on her mother's

side," Arnie offered. "The kids stayed at her place while Donna was at the hospital delivering the infant, Trisha."

Together, with the children between them, the two women walked out toward the car parked in the driveway—a Toyota Highlander hybrid.

"Where are they headed?" Jack asked. He knew Arnie had been listening remotely since Donna had risen to wake the children for school. As good as the audio reception was now, it would be even better once they broke into the house and bugged it.

"We've got a couple of hours. It's the kids' first day at their new school," Arnie explained. "Donna wants to walk them into their classrooms so that they can meet their teachers. Afterward, she and Phyllis are going grocery shopping, then to Costco and Home Depot." He paused to pop a stick of gum in his mouth. "Phyllis insists on staying with Donna for two weeks, or however long she feels she needs her, especially since Carl is 'out of town.'" He winced. "But she's ragging on Donna about Carl's lousy timing. Every time she does, Donna defends him. It's breaking my heart because she sounds as if she's going to cry."

"Enough already," Jack said gruffly. "It's beginning to sound like a regular soap opera."

Arnie sniffed. "Dude—have a heart!"

"Yeah, okay." Jack shrugged. The way his heart was pounding, he was surprised Arnie couldn't hear it, what with all the audio monitors in their house. "Having Phyllis here is both a curse and a blessing. Thank goodness they're leaving together. If Phyllis stayed behind, we wouldn't have this opportunity to drop a few bugs." He grabbed one of the two duffel bags with their gear. "Listen, any time Phyllis separates from Donna over the next few days, one of us should follow and try to strike up a conversation. She may not know anything, but then again, Donna may have confided in her about Carl's mood prior to the accident."

Arnie's eyes lit up. "Wow, great!" He grabbed the other bag. "Hey, can I wear a disguise? If it's in the park, I can pull off a bum easily."

"I don't doubt it in the least." Jack shook his head. "Just what we need—you getting arrested for panhandling Hilldale's fine citizens. Never mind. Let's get cracking in case they forgot the diaper bag again."

Arnie had already broken the passcode that armed the home's security system. They went into the garage and got into their car, then drove around the block until they were on the far side of the house. Then they climbed over the stone wall and into the backyard.

THE GOOD NEWS: THE BACK DOOR WAS EQUIPPED WITH A BUILT-in dog door.

The bad news: the Stones had a dog. A big dog. One that growled.

"Ryan forgot to mention this," Arnie muttered in a shaking voice.

"Turn around as you normally would, and go back to the house. Grab some of the packaged cheese out of the fridge," Jack suggested. "He'll love us in no time."

Arnie was gone in flash.

The dog, a blond collie, ran at his heels, barking.

Before a neighbor could come out to see what was

happening, Jack slipped in through the dog door, pulling one duffel in behind him, then the other.

A LOT OF THE STONES' THINGS WERE STILL IN BOXES.

This is going to make it virtually impossible for us to find the thumb drive, if it's here, Jack thought. As for the other intel that might have also been in Carl's possession, what form was it in—a file folder of papers? A microdot? Was it another thumb drive?

He came to the conclusion that the best place to start was the bedroom, and he walked upstairs. When he got there, from what he could tell, things were more organized. Clothes were hung in closets, or folded neatly in drawers. Linens were already stacked on the shelves.

He started with the dressers. The tall boy had to be Carl's. The top drawer was just deep enough to hold a man's wallet. Ties were laid out, flat, in rows. There were several small boxes that held cufflinks. Others held tie clips.

One slim box held four tickets to an upcoming Dodgers game. Apparently, Carl had planned on taking the family.

Jack doubted Donna would take them in his stead.

He opened the next drawer to find it equally divided between the dead man's socks and underwear. All were neatly folded. He sifted through the items with a gloved hand, feeling between them for anything hard and small, like the thumb drive, but finding nothing.

He repeated the search in the rest of the drawers, again finding nothing.

Then he moved on to Donna's dresser. It felt odd going

through the woman's unmentionables. Unlike her husband, her underwear was tossed in the drawer, willy-nilly. Like most of the women he knew, the garments came in all colors. While there were some more modest items, she owned a thong or two.

Or three or four.

And a pair of pink furry handcuffs.

Obviously, there's more to Mrs. Stone than meets the eye, he thought as he held up a white lace thong.

After going through the rest of her drawers with no success, he moved on to the closet. It was large, and the husband and wife were meant to share it—her dresses on one side, Carl's suits on the other.

He wondered how long Carl's things would hang there before Donna felt ready to part with them.

Until she got tired of crying herself to sleep each night.

He went through all the pockets, first of the suits and then of Donna's dresses and coats. No luck.

Donna's shoes were laid out, but Carl's shoes were still packed in boxes, on the deep top shelf, along with other boxes. He shifted one over. When he did, another fell. He cursed himself for his clumsiness. As he stacked the items back into the box, one caught his interest—

A portable gun vault.

It took a few moments to pick the lock. A Sig P250 was inside.

It must have been Donna's gun, since Carl had his with him at the end.

He hoped she knew how to use it.

~

While Arnie inserted audio bugs, Jack went through every room in search of the thumb drive. Besides looking in the obvious places—drawers, cabinets, bins, and pockets—he opened up jewelry and music boxes, searched books for cut-outs, felt through seams in the furniture, drapery, and into every nook and cranny he could find.

He came up with absolutely nothing.

When he was done, he assisted Arnie with replacing the down lighting domes with similar ones containing miniature webcams.

After every installation, Arnie tested each monitor's signal with an iPad. In between testing, he nibbled at a left-over casserole dish of chicken potpie that was on the counter. Lassie, who was now his new best friend, begged and whined at his feet.

"Hey, don't make too big of a dent in that pie," Jack warned him.

"But it's so good!" Arnie exclaimed with a full mouth. "Damn, this woman can cook! It's nothing like that store-bought crap our moms used to feed us as kids. Here, have a bite."

He held out his spoon.

Seeing this, Lassie leaped up on her back legs.

Surprised, Arnie jerked his arm away.

The casserole dish fell onto the floor.

Outside, the sound of a car could be heard, pulling into the drive.

"Oh...shit!" Arnie spit out potpie as he grabbed his duffel bag and headed for the dog door.

Jack rolled out behind him.

Lassie heard the car, too. Maybe she remembered her

primary allegiance was to the family, or maybe it was the potpie all over the kitchen floor, but in any case, she stayed put.

The men waited until Donna and her family were in the house before rolling the car back into the garage of the rental house across the street. Once they were inside, Arnie clicked on the webcam in time for him and Jack to see Donna scolding Lassie, and shooing her out the door.

"I feel guilty," Arnie admitted.

"You should," Jack chided him. "I hope it was worth it."

Arnie rubbed his stomach. "Heaven on a spoon. So, that's what it's like to have a good home-cooked meal! No wonder Carl married her."

Arnie would know better if he'd been the one rummaging through Donna's panty drawer.

So that he could get her white lace thong panty out of his mind, Jack quickly got to work.

"I THINK WE SHOULD GET A KID," ARNIE PROCLAIMED. HE'D just come back with the groceries, a.k.a., more beer and pizza.

Jack put down his binoculars to stare at him. "What are you, nuts?"

"No, I'm being serious," Arnie insisted. "Don't you see? If we had one, it would make it easier to talk to the neighbors—you know, at the park. Otherwise, I'm just the sad sack neighbor guy tossing a Frisbee to myself."

In a way, he's got a point, Jack conceded.

"Great. I'll ask Ryan to requisition one for us."

Arnie frowned. "Really?"

"No, you moron. What are you going to feed a kid, beer and pizza?" He pointed to the countertop, where Arnie had left their primary food supply. "Should we ask Ryan to spring for another cot, too?"

"Okay, I get the point. Then, how about a midget who just acts like a kid?"

Jack's reaction was to sigh and rub the headache from his forehead.

"The least we can get is a dog," Arnie pointed out.

"No." Jack shook his head adamantly. "With a dog comes...responsibility." And that was something neither of them could take on if they were to focus on taking down the Quorum.

So no dog, and no kid.

And certainly no wife.

It had been two weeks since the twenty-four hour surveillance mission had begun. So far, Arnie's attempts to engage the neighbors had resulted in three slaps to his face. Either his disguises weren't working or he had lousy social skills, or both. Jack was willing to bet on Door Number Three.

In Arnie's favor, he had been invited to a neighborhood key party. His reconnaissance brought both of them some interesting insights into a more provocative point of view of life in the suburbs, to say the least. "One thing's for sure, there are a lot of unhappy couples in Hilldale."

In time, would that have described Donna and Carl?

In the hours when Jack wasn't on surveillance duty, he did what he could to delve into files covering every facet of Carl's life, both before and during his tenure with Acme—

the background check on his parents, his academic reports, his military record, and Acme's recruitment and training reports.

Nothing stood out.

Jack then combed over the dead agent's mission reports, looking for any telltale sign that might indicate when he knew the Quorum was onto him. He found none. The reports were perfunctory at best—no color or embellishments. On the rare times Carl's reports included clandestine surveillance photos of the Quorum operatives who had interacted with him, they were either targets who had been exterminated or who had been apprehended in the meantime.

However, there were no photos of his Quorum recruiter and handler, a man named Eric Weber.

Nor were there any of Tatyana Zakharov, although one of his earlier filings reported a brief encounter, apparently by mistake. Carl's description of her was straightforward and spot on, matching Jack's own observations:

Beautiful. Smart. Deadly.

Now in hindsight, Jack wondered if Carl's assessment of her was short and not so sweet for personal reasons.

There was no picture of Pinky Ring either. This was particularly disappointing to Jack because there was a fifty-fifty chance the man would have been identified by name as well.

Going over all these, Ryan was adamant that Carl never let on that he felt his cover was blown. "He knew I'd pull him out at the first sign of danger."

"He must have been worried about something," Jack

insisted. "Why else would he have left his family in that bunker of a house?"

A house in which his bereaved widow slept fitfully, if she slept at all.

Maybe the Quorum figured out that the intel died along with Carl, Jack reasoned.

To date, there hadn't been any break-in attempts or other unusual activity in or around the house. Life for the Stones— and for Jack and Arnie, for that matter—was settling into a pattern.

On most days now, it was Aunt Phyllis who took Mary and Jeff to school and then went on to the stores for any necessary shopping. During that time, Donna cared for infant Trisha, and did the laundry or other housework. Usually Phyllis got home in time for Trisha's mid-morning nap, at which time Donna took a run, or she slipped off to the shooting range.

Jack was impressed with what he saw—clean shots, mostly bull's-eyes.

It relieved him to know that, on some level, she could protect herself and her family.

Unlike her days, which were filled with family tasks that kept her grounded in the present instead of lost in the past, Donna's nights were spent roaming from room to room in the large house. If she wasn't patting the heads of her sleeping children, she was staring out the great room window facing the backyard and into the dark recesses beyond the trees.

Or she was baking—cinnamon rolls, cakes, pies, cookies.

And all the while, she cried.

It's odd—what people will do as they mourn, Jack

thought. He laughed mercilessly as he thought about his own recent actions in light of his wife leaving him.

He'd thrown himself into his work.

In other words, despite his anger and sadness, he hadn't changed a thing about his life.

I have lousy priorities, he realized. I guess Carl did, too. If I'd had his family and knew that the Quorum was after me, I would have run for the hills with them, and never looked back.

9

Ambush

The best ambushes create a diversion first, so that the target is looking in the wrong place when the time is right.

Even if you're the target, you can turn the tables on your aggressors by taking the first opportunity to take them off guard.

If possible, have this interaction in the presence of others. No one wants witnesses to a hit.

"Ouch! Trouble in paradise," Arnie murmured.

It was ten-thirty on the fourth Wednesday of their surveillance mission. Jack looked up from the file he was reading and walked over to the wall in front of the el-shaped couch, where Arnie had set up a seventy-inch flat screen monitor. The screen was divided into six separate webcam feeds. Like dominos, every ten seconds the sections changed to another location in the surveillance area not previously seen in the past sixty seconds.

He scanned the screens, one by one. "Where should I be looking? Have you spotted an intruder?" Jack's hand went instinctively to his gun holster.

"No, no! Nothing like that. It's just a trio of the neighborhood mean mommies." Arnie swiped one of the screens so that it grew twice as large as the other ones, and moved front and center. It showed the Stones' driveway. A Mercedes G wagon was pulling up.

When it stopped, three women exited from the vehicle. Their attire was casual: slim jeans and silk blouses under casual linen jackets that were cut in a way that fit their well-toned bodies like gloves. They wore jeweled sandals with heels as high as those Jack had seen on Vegas showgirls.

Jack stared at Arnie. "You know these women?"

"Sure, everyone does…well, I mean, if you hang out at the playground, you pick up the gossip."

Jack snorted. "Don't keep me in suspense."

"Let's just say they rule the school—and I mean that, literally. The brunette is Tiffy Swift, and the redhead is Hayley Coxhead. See the tall blonde, in the lead? Her name is *Penelope Bing*." Arnie looked at Jack, as if the name should mean something to him.

Jack shrugged helplessly.

"Her son, Cheever, is in Jeff's classroom. He's a bit of a brat. But since Penelope is the head of the Hilldale Elementary School PTA, she has clout at the school. The last time his teacher sent an email to Penelope 'Bada' Bing—that's what some of the mothers call her, because she's like a mafia don —the poor woman was suspended by the principal."

Both men watched as the front door opened. Donna was dressed for her jog—a loose T-shirt over a sports bra, and cropped yoga pants. Trisha was strapped to her chest. There was a baby blanket over Donna's shoulder. From the looks of things, she was in the middle of breastfeeding Trisha.

Arnie turned beet red.

"Oh, wow! Ladies, to what do I owe this honor?" Donna asked. Her voice sounded harried.

Jack enlarged the screen so that they could better see and hear what was happening in the living room.

A basket of unfolded laundry was at the foot of the sofa. Using one hand to secure Trisha, she scooped up a batch of folded towels off the sofa with the other.

The women exchanged knowing smirks.

"We're not interrupting something, I hope?" Penelope asked. Her voice dripped of false sweetness.

"No, nothing at all." Donna smiled back, but her voice was brittle as ice.

Good girl, Jack thought.

"Please, have a seat while I put Trisha down for her nap." She nodded toward the sofa before walking upstairs with the baby.

While she was gone, the women perused the living room. Besides the laundry scattered about, there were still a few unopened boxes—mostly Carl's old baseball trophies, which she didn't yet have the heart to display, let alone put in the garage—and an upturned box of Legos by the fireplace, left from the night before, when Jeff was in the middle of building a castle.

The woman named Hayley whispered to the others, "She's not much of a housekeeper, is she?"

"Maybe that's why her husband hasn't been home since she moved in, over a month ago," Tiffy muttered.

"Ahem!" The other two women were so busy exchanging snickers that they hadn't noticed Donna was standing in the foyer behind them until Penelope cleared her throat. "So, Mrs. Stone—May I call you Donna?—I don't know if you remember because you rushed out the door so fast after the PTA new parent's tea, but I'm Penelope Bing, the PTA president."

"Yes, of course I remember you, and your co-vice chairs as well, Hayley and Tiffy."

"Yes, well one thing you conveniently forgot was to sign up for a volunteer duty." Penelope practically clicked her tongue in mock horror. "That being said, we assigned one for you—cafeteria duty, every Friday."

"Ah! I see. I'm sorry, but that won't be convenient for me, since I have an infant." She pointed upstairs. "Perhaps there's some task I can do at home?"

"If you'd stuck around instead leaving before the meeting was over, you would have had a lot of other tasks to choose from," Hayley scolded her. "So the short answer is 'no.'"

Donna cast her eyes at the ground. "I'll see if I can work around it."

Jack couldn't believe his ears. "Why would she let those bitches walk all over her?"

Arnie threw up his hands. "I told you—they can seriously make her life miserable!"

"With the hell she's been through, she doesn't need any more misery—"

Arnie shushed Jack. "Wait—Penelope just said something about Jeff."

They both turned back toward the screen.

"—and my little Cheever says that Jeff is really good at T-Ball."

Donna nodded. "Carl—his father—played ball in college." She glanced away quickly.

Jack zoomed in on her face. Her eyes glistened with tears.

"We can't wait to meet him," Hayley said slyly. "In fact, my husband and I are having a dinner party next Saturday. Just a small, intimate group. We hope you can make it."

Donna opened her mouth to say something, only to hesitate before murmuring, "He's...out of town. I'll be flying solo—if that's okay."

Hayley scowled. "Tell you what, why don't we make it another time, when it's more convenient for both of you?"

Donna forced a smile onto her face. "I'm sure he'd appreciate that as well." She stood up. "Please excuse me for being such a bad hostess! I've just baked a chocolate walnut pie. Why don't we have some? I've also brewed a fresh pot of coffee—hazelnut. I'll be right back with both, okay?"

Before they could say no, she glided off to the kitchen.

"That's more like it," Penelope muttered. "I swear! You have to crack a whip with these newbies. Otherwise, they'll run all over you."

"I'll bet the husband has a secret life, somewhere else in the country." Hayley raised a brow. "You know, a *bigamist*."

Tiffy's mouth fell open. "You mean, he might be in the Ku Klux Klan?"

"No, you idiot!" Penelope hissed. "That's a bigot! A bigamist has two wives."

Jack couldn't take it anymore. He switched the largest screen on the monitor to the kitchen, where Donna was patting her tears away with a white linen napkin. When she was done, she folded it alongside three others on the tray in front of her, which also held four elegantly patterned plates and the same number of dessert forks.

When she raised her head, her eyes were cold as steel.

In no time at all, she cut the pie on the counter into healthy wedges, and shoveled one onto each plate. Next, she poured real cream into a silver creamer that matched a sugar bowl holding white cubes. Finally, she took the pot of the fresh brew and poured it into an elaborate coffee urn.

Then she did something odd: she went to one of the cabinets, reached in, and pulled out a box of Chocolate Ex-Lax. She opened the wrapper, broke off six cubes, and shaved them over three of the wedges, which she warmed up for a minute in the microwave before placing them back on the tray.

Arnie's jaw dropped "Is she really going to—"

Jack was laughing so hard that he fell off the couch.

Before lifting the tray and walking back into the living room, Donna's demure smile was back in place.

Her visitors ooohed and ahhhed over her plates, her wonderful coffee and of course her exceptionally delicious pie. But within twenty minutes, Tiffy's face was green. Penelope didn't look well, either. She stood up abruptly and announced she had to run—now.

Donna walked the women to the front door, which they bolted through, barely acknowledging her as Penelope revved the engine, put the car in reverse, and screeched out of the driveway.

When Arnie swiped the screen so that it that gave them a bird's eye view of the streets of Hilldale, Jack realized the tech op had tied their surveillance grid to Acme's satellite as well. Arnie zoomed in on Penelope's car, which was now careening to a halt in front of what must have been Tiffy's house, because both she and Hayley jumped out quickly and ran to the front door. Tiffy was furiously rummaging in her purse for her keys while Penelope zoomed off to her own home, three blocks over.

"I wonder what she would have done if one of them had threatened her kids?"

Jack frowned. "Um...rat poison?"

From the look on Arnie's face, he guessed they were thinking the same thing:

Donna Stone was not a woman to mess with.

Jack was beginning to see her in a new light.

A RUSTLING SOUND WAS COMING FROM THE TREE HOUSE.

It was eleven at night, it couldn't be the kids, Jack thought. He swiped the screen containing that specific feed, so that it enlarged.

Yes, there was someone up there.

Damn it, one of the kids must have hung a net filled with stuffed animals directly over the camera in there, because his view of the person was hazy at best.

From another camera that was hung from an outdoor light so that it captured the rest of the backyard, Jack could make out Donna, moving slowly toward the tree house.

Apparently, she'd heard it, too.

When she was right below the tree house, she stopped.

His heart leaped into his throat. She could be walking

right into a trap. If so, she'd be helpless. From what he could see, she hadn't armed herself.

When she started climbing the ladder, he reached for his gun. He shook Arnie, who was sprawled out on the couch, grabbing a few Z's. "Hey! Quick! Get up and watch the monitors. Someone's in the tree house and I'm going to investigate."

Arnie leaped straight up and stumbled toward the monitor, as Jack hustled to the front door.

"Jack, wait!" Arnie hissed. "Listen!"

Jack stopped.

"I miss Daddy," a tiny voice said.

Mary.

Donna heaved a sigh. "I know, honey I miss him, too."

"He's been gone so long this time! Too long! When was the last time he called, Mommy?"

"Why...the other night. It was after midnight, and you were sleeping so soundly that I didn't want to wake you—"

Hearing that, Mary's sobs got louder. Jack and Arnie listened to some slams and thumps as Donna said, "Mary, please don't hit me! Can't you see I'm hurting, too?"

Now they were both crying.

Through the webcam, Jack and Arnie could barely make out two figures huddled together in the tree house.

Through her choked sobs, Mary whispered, "I don't care what time it is! I just want to say hello. I want to tell him I love him! And to tell him—to tell him that if he loved me, *he'd keep his promise to me, and come back.*"

Neither said anything for a while.

Finally Mary said, "I'm sorry."

"Don't...don't be. It's not your fault."

It's mine, Jack thought.

"Mommy—sometimes I forget what Daddy looks like."

"Shhhhhh," she whispered. "Let's picture him together now."

It was half an hour before mother and daughter rose to their feet. Mary went down the ladder first. When Donna reached the ground after her, she put her hand in Mary's, and together, they walked to the back door.

"Jeez, do you think she can go the distance with her role in this mission?" Arnie wondered out loud.

Jack shook his head. "I don't know. It would help if we knew whether the Quorum already had the intel. That way, we'd know for certain if she's a target in the first place."

Several minutes later, Jack heard Donna rustling in her bedroom.

She was sobbing again.

He stayed up until she fell asleep.

10

Compromised

An operation, asset, or agent is said to be compromised when he or she has been uncovered by a competing entity, and therefore no longer secret.

Should the undercover operation also take place in bed—that is, under the covers—the situation could be called a compromising position.

Another reason to stay away from an agent provocateur.

DONNA STONE'S RUNS USUALLY STAYED WITHIN A FIVE-MILE loop through Hilldale's wide, winding streets.

At first, Jack did his best to keep up with her on foot, but because he worried she'd feel a presence behind her, he now followed by car, some four or five blocks behind.

He'd pull over if he felt he was getting too close for comfort, wait for her to sprint ahead, then follow again.

He could have sent Arnie to follow her, but he chose to

take on this task himself. As much as he tried to convince himself that his reason for shadowing her had to do with making sure she wasn't abducted, he knew better.

The truth was, simply, he loved watching her.

Somewhere into the fourth week of surveillance, he realized he wasn't just tracking her movements and that of her children, but he was actually studying her.

In truth, she fascinated him.

In so many ways, she was aware of her surroundings. When it came to her children, she had a sixth sense as to their needs, whether it was a bottle for Trisha, or a gentle admonishment for Mary before some infraction caused her to lose some much-desired privilege. At the same time, he wondered why her intuition had failed her when it came to Carl.

Granted, she'd been married to a master spy.

Perhaps her deep love for him had blinded her to the obvious.

He had no such excuse.

After all, he *was* the master spy.

Having now studied her for hours on end, he knew every angle of her face, and every curve of her body. He had replayed all the video footage and audio recordings they'd collected of her so many times that he could read every inflection in her voice, the nuance in her every move.

Perhaps in his analysis of her, he'd find the cause of the blind spot to his own marriage.

In fact, he couldn't remember the last time he'd thought of his ex.

He no longer dreamt of her.

Now he dreamt of Donna.

He felt guilty about it—not because, in his mind, he could see he was capable of moving beyond the pain of his loss, but because he knew she wasn't.

He also could not deny the role he played in Carl's death.

Maybe it was time for him to leave.

Suddenly, and for the first time since he'd been following her, she took a different route entirely: onto a trail managed by the National Parks Service that bordered the far end of Hilldale.

He cursed himself for leaving the house in shorts, as opposed to sweats. His sunglasses and baseball cap would give him some cover, as would two week's growth of stubble.

Hell, what was he worried about? At the speed she was going, he'd be proud of himself if he could just keep up with her.

Like most of that part of the coast, the trail roamed coastal headlands and through marsh woods. Every now and again, it would meander through a crowd of scraggly bushes, but for the most part they were traipsing through dry grass.

Her daily runs made it easier for her to climb up the next hill, which was crowned with a copse of tall oaks. He slowed up naturally. But two-thirds of the way to the top, he was so worried he'd lose her that he sprinted over it—

And over her as well.

Apparently, she'd bent down to tie her shoe.

He couldn't stop fast enough to avoid her, somersaulting over her.

He landed hard, and facedown. His head hit a rock.

He didn't know how long he'd blacked out. But when he came to, she was standing over him.

"I'm...I'm so sorry! Are you alright?"

He turned his head before speaking. Dropping his voice into a lower register, he answered, "Yeah. Fine. Sorry."

He covered his face with his hand, but it wasn't part of the act. Warm blood was dripping from a cut above his left eye, which was blurry. He scrambled to his feet and grabbed his sunglasses, which had landed further down the path.

Seeing the blood, she instantly reached out to comfort him. Realizing what she was about to do, he jerked his head away. He stumbled to his feet and started back down the hill, the way they had come.

On the drive home, he tried not to think of what he would have done had she touched him.

He knew the answer: He would have taken her, right then and there.

He knew it was time for him to go, but he'd be damned if he'd leave her.

Ever.

"What you did was stupid, and could have compromised the whole damn mission." Ryan's voice was still at a reasonable decibel level, but his tone was as chilling as an iceberg.

Jack resisted the urge to take the bag of ice he held to his eye and toss it at Ryan. "How was I supposed to know that she'd stop to tie her shoe?"

"You shouldn't have been following her, anyway. It should have been Arnie—with one of his crazy disguises."

"Are you kidding? A typical jog for her is five miles, minimum! He would have passed out after the first quarter-mile."

"I've got to get that boy into a gym," Ryan conceded with a nod. "In fact, it's time to yank both of you off surveillance. I need Arnie back on Tech Ops, and I need you on an important extermination. Consider this your penance for the lost files paid in full...Okay, not in full. Until they show up, you'll always be my bitch."

"What? But...Don't pull me off now! Look, Ryan, if it's because of my accident—"

Ryan frowned. "To some extent, yes, that has something to do with it. Now that she's seen your face, your role in this mission has been compromised."

"But...but she didn't! I swear!" Jack hated the fact he was stuttering like some foolish schoolboy with a hard-on.

"You don't know that. By your own admission, you were out cold, at least for a few seconds." Ryan slapped the desk in disgust. "Listen, even if she hasn't seen it, I can't afford having my best hard man babysitting a decoy."

"That's all she is to you—a decoy?" Jack muttered.

"No. She's also a woman I have tremendous respect for. And she's also the widow of one of my agents." Ryan hesitated, as if searching for the right words. "Jack, I know you feel guilty about Carl. We've all made mistakes we regret—mistakes that have fatal repercussions. But maybe this isn't the best way for you to make amends. If you want to catch the Quorum, you can't wait until it comes to you. Right now, I need you in the field."

Jack knew he was right.

If I hadn't fallen in love with her, I would have been itching for a transfer by now.

Yes, okay I admit it—*I love Donna Stone.*

I just can't tell her.

And now, I won't be here, watching over her.

He looked over to Ryan. "I presume you'll still keep a surveillance team on her."

Ryan nodded. "I owe that much to Carl. So yes—at least until we hear affirmatively that the Quorum did somehow retrieve what they've been looking for and she's in the clear, or until we take down the Quorum. I'm hoping for the best result, the latter of those two."

They shook hands before Jack started out the door.

He had no doubt that Ryan knew why they were shaking —to seal his commitment to keep watch over Donna and her children.

"CAN I HAVE A TABLE OUT ON THE DECK?" JACK ASKED THE hostess at the Sand Dollar.

She looked down at the seating chart on the podium in front of her. "I'm sorry, sir, but it looks like every table is taken." Her apology came with a smile.

"I see an empty one, right there—the corner one, by the railing." He pointed through the reception area window, where the deck could be seen clearly.

"Oh..." She looked down at the chart again. "I'm sorry, but that one is reserved, and it's marked 'special occasion.' It will be occupied in about fifteen minutes." She seemed sincerely sorry she couldn't give him the table he wanted.

Hoping to make it up to him, she scanned the chart with her finger, only to show the futility of his wish by shrugging helplessly. "If you care to wait for an outside table, there may be one opening up, but it looks like it'll be at least another forty minutes."

He shook his head. He was famished, and he desperately needed a drink.

The restaurant was his last stop in Orange County before heading out to LAX.

"Tell you what, I'll get you the next best thing—an inside table overlooking the patio."

Yeah sure, what the hell, he thought. Seeing his nod put an even bigger smile on her lips. She beckoned him to follow her.

From what he could see from the neighboring tables, the surf and turf looked good, so he ordered it too. The tumbler of Scotch held a generous pour. By the time he had it in his hand, the table on the patio was indeed occupied.

By Donna.

What was she doing there?

Then he remembered: *today would have been her anniversary with Carl.*

She sat by herself, staring out at the setting sun, already half below the horizon.

The wind was gentle enough that she hadn't noticed how her shawl now dipped below her bare shoulder. The strapless sundress was a soft beige, almost the color of her skin.

It took only a few moments before the sun dipped below the water line. After watching the last of its rays fade into a darkening sky, she turned back to face the table.

A tear glistened on her cheek.

He wished he were beside her to nudge it away. To tell her not to worry, that all would be fine.

To tell her that he loved her.

There were too many reasons why he couldn't, the first and foremost being the reason why she was there in the first place:

She still loved Carl.

He motioned the waitress. "See the pretty lady out there? Send over a glass of your best cab." Before the woman could ask, he added, "And tell her it's on the house."

He didn't wait for his meal.

When he rose, he left more than enough cash to cover the Scotch, the surf-and-turf, a glass of the cabernet, and a generous tip.

He caught his plane with time to spare.

11

Double Agents

If you're able to turn a target into an asset or an operative, you've got yourself a double agent.

If your enemy is able to coerce one of your agents or assets to feed them intel on you, he's got a double agent.

Here's hoping your double agent lets you in on the secret before his double agent tells him about yours.

"Are you with the band?" Two groupies, sunning themselves topless on the poolside chaises outside the Miami Setei Hotel's penthouse suite, posed the question in unison.

If only, Jack thought. And twins, no less. I should have never sold my drum set. "Nope, sorry. I'm a journalist—with *Esquire*."

As if *that* gave him an inkling of cred.

"Oh," they sighed, obviously disappointed. They flipped over on their stomachs.

He lowered his head and tilted it sideways for a better view of the two comely backsides. Their bright blue bikinis exposed identical beauty marks on their left butt cheeks.

He exhaled slowly. Um…yeah, definitely twins.

Damn it, a better cover would have been *People*, maybe, or *US Weekly*. Nope, a *Playboy* photographer ID would have worked even better. He made a mental note to see if Ryan could arrange that next time.

"The dude may be old but, hell, bitches—you can still take him in the back and show him a good time," Mass Reconstruction's lead singer, Rory McManus, shouted from the penthouse's master bedroom.

Old? Jack knew for a fact the musician was a year older than him. He was tempted to shoot Rory, right then and there. But no, that would have defeated the purpose of Jack's mission:

To learn how, and where Rory was passing firearms of all kinds—pistols, rifles, semi-automatic assault rifles, even tanks—to Sudanese rebel forces.

Once he had the needed intel, he could shoot him. Hopefully with one of Rory's own guns.

Of course, he'd make it look like an accident. It was no secret that Rory was a pothead, or that he had depression issues, and that he liked to play Russian roulette with a loaded barrel.

The truth of the matter was that Rory was the worst kind of gun enthusiast. He had more money than brains and more guns than he could possibly handle, let alone remember he owned. So yeah, he was certainly an NRA poster boy. No issues there, as long as the firearms he acquired were permissible to own in the US, and that he purchased them legally.

That was the problem. As one of the world's highest paid entertainers, he had unlimited finances to buy as many toys as he could possibly want, in any country he wanted, and take them home on his private jet.

To top it off, his arsenal was growing at an astonishing rate.

But he wasn't into hunting. He was into ego. He was into playing God.

His benevolence extended to those who came looking for whatever firearms he'd grown tired of—as long as they paid tribute with an open pocketbook.

Fortified by a half-dozen Patron Premium shots and enveloped in a cannabis haze, he'd been recorded declaring, "Yo, this music gig won't last forever. At my burn rate, I lose money every time I go on the road. Brokering arms is my retirement pension, yo."

If one of his buyers was astute enough to know the name of his latest hit or at least one of his golden oldies, he'd throw in a concert ticket with a backstage pass, or an old school CD.

Because that was how he rolled.

No thought at all about the many innocent civilians his castoffs had murdered, including the one who eventually recorded him making that statement—Sally Maxwell, the international runway model and ever-present arm charm to Mass Reconstruction's lead singer.

It had always been Jack Craig's contention Sally was too

young, too beautiful, and too green to be an effective Acme asset. There was absolutely nothing covert about her.

He had to admit, though, that she was also one of the smartest people he'd ever recruited. That, and the fact that Rory was obsessed with her, trumped her liabilities.

"With all he's handling, there's no way he's the middle man here. He's got to be acting as a front for someone," Jack had explained to Sally. "Can you find out who's supplying him?"

"I'll do my best," she promised. As she handed Jack the thumb drive with the recording, she murmured, "The bigger the gun, the smaller the dick."

He nodded. "Oh, by the way, did I tell you I carry a SwissMini C1ST?" He held his thumb and index finger apart by just two inches.

To this day, he still remembered her hoarse belly laugh at his expense.

And he would never forget the look on the face of her corpse.

There wasn't much left of the rest of her skull.

He flew down to Jamaica the moment he heard of the shooting—in one of the hotel rooms rented by Mass Reconstruction for the band and its crew. The coroner ruled the death a suicide, based on the fact that she'd been shot at close range: the hollow-point bullet entered on the right side of her head, just above her ear.

The gun was Rory's, of course.

At least the detectives had video-recorded Rory's testimony. Through crocodile tears, he choked out an explanation with as many holes in it as his designer-ripped T-shirt. "She did too much of your great ganja, bros. But then she went into a downer, yo, so I left her alone to hang with some of my homies out by the pool. The next thing we know —bam! I go running in, and there's brains splattered all over the joint."

He had no explanation why there wasn't any gun residue on her hands.

They never tested his hands for any residue, either.

Besides that, Sally was a leftie.

Based on the evidence Sally had secured prior to her death, Acme's client, the ATF, had no problem with ridding itself of yet another illegal arms dealer. Considering his high profile, the only caveat was that the extermination was to look like an accidental death, or a suicide.

Jack was only too happy to oblige.

The musician had a sound check in a couple of hours. Jack's *Esquire* reporter cover allowed him an hour, maybe two, with the asshole, so Jack would have to work fast.

He was willing to bet his target was already halfway through the stash of white rhino he'd purchased from one of the roadies just last night. Between it, and a few drops of Russian truth drug SP-117 in his perennially present Red Bull, Rory would be loose enough for Jack to lead the conversation into any direction he wanted.

After he got the answers he was looking for, Rory would suffer a heart attack, thanks to a prick from a needle containing a super-condensed dosage of succinylcholine, hidden in the underside of the fake fraternity ring on Jack's right hand.

Whereas Rory's penthouse suite in the Setei Hotel took up the whole top floor—the fortieth—the other band members' rooms were on the floor beneath their lead singer.

Jack had also booked a room, not under his name or the *Esquire* reporter pseudonym of Anders Zorn, but a different alias and disguise altogether—Steve Stover. As Stover, he had arrived a few days before the band, and was scheduled to leave a few days after, as would any single guy vacationing in South Beach and on the prowl for fun in the sun. The hotel's hallway security webcam was running a recorded loop in which no one was in the hallway. A ghost loop will also play on the penthouse elevator loop, until Jack had cleared the building. Should anything go wrong during or immediately after the extermination, he could use the room as a safe house.

Hopefully, he wouldn't have to.

He knocked on the bedroom door.

"What are you waiting for, dude, a written invitation?" Rory's laugh rolled into a cannabis cough. "Quit eyeing my sluts and come on in. What's your name again? My fucking press bitch left it for me in a message, but I'm too stoned to remember."

"Anders Zorn," Jack murmured.

Sally, this one's for you.

"YOU LOOK LIKE YOU'VE SEEN A GHOST, YO," RORY LAUGHED through a smoke ring. Then he turned to where the reporter was staring:

At the raven-haired groupie in the bed beside him.

She was staring back at the reporter, too.

Then she laughed.

Then Tatyana Zakharov pulled a gun.

Rory got the bullet—up close, to the temple.

When she turned around, Jack's gun was on her temple —up close.

"Don't worry," she said sweetly to Jack, "He was a righty, and I'm on his right."

Jack dug the gun into her temple with one hand, and yanked her gun out of her hand with his other, pocketing it. "You told Rory to kill Sally Maxwell, didn't you?"

She snorted. "Who, Rory? Ha! He didn't have the guts. He's all talk, no action. Just like he was in bed." She held the pinky of her right hand straight out, only to let it curl down. "The fucking braggart. He told her too much, let her see everything. She had to go."

Jack grabbed her by the throat and slammed her into the striped mahogany headboard. "The Quorum is an arms supplier, isn't it?"

"Clever man! Go to the head of the class." She smiled up at him.

"And the little cretin who came with you, at Leonid Romanov's party, put the plastic explosives under Carl Stone's car that killed him, didn't he? Because you found out he'd infiltrated your organization?"

She stared at him, then burst out laughing. "My, my! We have all the answers, now don't we? If you're so smart, Mr. Craig, then enlighten me—who do you think has the files you've misplaced?"

"Oh. My. *Gawd*!" the twins screamed, in unison.

Instinctively, Jack turned to where the two girls stood—in the threshold of the sliding door leading out to the pool.

In that short moment, Tatyana smacked the gun out of his hand.

It fell on the floor, landing at the feet of the twins.

Tatyana grabbed her gun from Jack's pocket. Rising to her feet, she pointed it at his chest.

One of them picked up Jack's gun. Her hand shook so hard that a bullet ricocheted as she pointed it at Tatyana, then at Jack, then back to Tatyana.

"Brittney, sweetheart, hand me the gun, before you hurt someone—or yourself." Tatyana's voice was gentle, but firm.

"Brittney, don't do it! She'll shoot you," Jack insisted.

"Whitney, what should I do?" the girl whimpered.

The other girl frowned. "I never liked her. Whenever she came around, we were Rory's sloppy seconds."

Tatyana sighed. And shot Britney in the chest.

As she fell back, the gun dropped to the floor.

Jack lunged for it, tackling Whitney to the floor with him. He grabbed the gun, and rolled behind a chair, taking aim at the bed—

Tatyana wasn't there.

She'd gone out the door.

"Stay here," he commanded the whimpering girl as he ran out of the room.

Tatyana made it all the way to the elevator, and frantically pushed the DOWN button. The doors were just closing as Jack got off a shot.

He pounded the OPEN button with his fist, but it was already headed down, directly to the lobby.

He couldn't let her get away. He had to find out what she meant when she taunted him about the missing intel. Maybe it hadn't blown up with Carl after all.

But if that were the case, where was it?

He ran to the fire exit, and down the steps to the thirty-eighth floor and got on an elevator there, skipping the thirty-ninth floor so as not to run into any of Rory's entourage. He knew where the elevator's webcam was placed and made sure not to show his face to it.

When the elevator slowed to open on the twelfth floor, he slammed his hand against the wall. A couple was standing in front of the doors. They were kissing, as if they had all the time in the world.

To hell with that. He pushed the lobby button again—hard. "Sorry, this elevator is full," he declared.

The doors shut on their surprised faces.

His prayers were answered, and the rest of the ride was a straight shot to the lobby.

When the doors finally opened on the lobby level, he strolled casually toward the penthouse elevator door and pushed the button—

It was coming up from the underground parking garage.

Shit—she's down there, he thought to himself. He walked as fast as he could, out of the lobby, and down into the garage, through the vehicle exit lane.

No cars were headed toward him. He walked briskly toward the penthouse elevator.

It was open.

It was empty.

A wide streak of blood led to an empty parking space.

Somehow, she had driven away.

He tapped on his cell, calling Arnie's direct line.

He answered on the first ring. "Whazzup, dude?"

"Clean up on aisle five," he muttered.

He paused, then asked, "How many cans?"

"Two. And one…rolled away."

"I see. Let me guess—I'm supposed to check every doghouse, outhouse, steakhouse, lake house—"

"Just the emergency rooms." He gulped for air. "Female, late twenties, Caucasian, long dark hair—almost black. One bullet wound. Tell the boss man it's Tatyana. Just in case the bullet wasn't fatal, there should be an APB put out on her." He winced when he thought of Whitney. "Oh yeah, and there's a witness. Her name is Whitney. She's one of the band's groupies. The shooter killed her twin sister in front of her, so she should be able to give a good description of her—and of me too, unfortunately."

"Don't worry, I'm on it," Arnie murmured, then hung up.

Jack ran to his car.

He pulled out just as the black-and-whites were pulling up.

ARNIE'S CALL CAME JUST AS JACK HIT THE STREET. "THERE'S A woman matching Tatyana's description found in a car. It looks like she was trying to make it to Mount Sinai on Miami Beach." He paused. "She didn't."

"Can we get a photo ID from the hospital morgue?"

"I tried. When the morgue attendant went to check, he said the body had been checked out."

"Damn it! By whom?"

"Apparently, someone with Federal clearance. But it wasn't anyone here. Ryan is checking with our client, to see if it was someone there. I'll keep you in the loop." He clicked off.

She must have known she wasn't going to make it, and notified the Quorum to send a cleaner, he thought.

That night, on the plane back to Paris, he dreamt he told Donna about Tatyana.

She was so happy, she cried.

Then she kissed him.

When he woke up, he could have sworn it all happened.

ONE YEAR LATER

12

Enigma

The word, enigma, means riddle, or puzzle.

During World War II, Nazi Germany created a roto-cipher machine called Enigma, as a way of coding and deciphering messages. This was first discovered by one of its enemies — Poland, with the help of mathematicians from France. When Great Britain entered the war, Enigma cryptology went into full gear.

It provided the intel that helped in winning the war.

It's much easier to break a machine-made code than to decipher the emotions and feelings of a human. Machines may be able to calculate outcomes, but most humans act first and think later.

Sadly, the end result isn't always what we hope.

We are the ultimate enigma.

JACK WAS UP FOR RYAN'S SUGGESTION THAT THEY BREAK BREAD

at Duke's Malibu restaurant. The food was great, the dress code was casual, the patrons were laid back, for the most part, and it was far enough north on the PCH that it didn't attract the tourist flow from the Santa Monica strip.

By the time Jack got there, Ryan was already seated at one of the inside tables near a window—a great place to be as the sun set below the horizon. Jack knew Ryan would have asked that their order be put on the grill the moment he walked through the door. The menu was small, and those who came knew to order the catch of the day—seared rare and rubbed raw with seven spices—along with the grilled Brussels sprouts, and a hunk of the hula pie for dessert. Case closed.

Ryan beckoned Jack over, then tapped his glass to the waitress and held up two fingers. She nodded and by the time Jack had reached the table, she was at his side with a tumbler of Johnny Walker Blue.

When he smiled at her, she blushed.

Ryan laughed. "Does it ever get old?"

Jack looked at him, puzzled. "What do you mean?"

"You know—the effect you have on women."

Jack shrugged. "You didn't call me here to talk about my love life."

"You're right. In fact, it's the last thing to do with what I've got to ask you." He placed his napkin in his lap. "However, you're close enough to the subject that you may have some useful insights."

"Sure, what's up?"

Ryan looked him in the eye. "I'd like to ask Donna to work for us."

"Say that again?" The place was buzzing with talk and

laughter, not to mention the crash of the waves just outside the window, so it seemed to Jack that he had good reason to ask Ryan to repeat himself, when in reality he'd heard his boss perfectly well.

He just hadn't liked what he'd heard.

"I said I'd like to ask Donna to work for us." Ryan popped a Brussels sprout into his mouth. "What do you think about that idea?"

Jack stared out at the water for a moment while he tried to think of a way to back Ryan off this harebrained scheme without seeming unprofessional, or worse yet, irrational about it.

Not to mention, the last thing Jack wanted was for Ryan to realize he'd fallen in love with a woman he'd never formally met. "I...I think it's crazy. And stupid. She's a wild card! She's—"

Ryan nodded thoughtfully. "Yeah, I agree. I'm doing it."

Jack put down his glass with a thud. "Didn't you hear what I just said?"

"Yes. But you're not talking from your head, you're talking from your dick."

"What the hell do you mean by that?"

"We all have our reasons as to why we're here, Jack. If you were to be honest with yourself, you're primarily here for the exact same reason that Donna would join us: to avenge a loss."

"Okay yeah, I'll admit it. I'm out for blood. But two wrongs don't make a right. Remember that old proverb?"

"Of course I do. Here's another golden chestnut: try it, you'll like it."

Jack frowned. "That's an old ad slogan—for Alka-

Seltzer." Something he could use, right about now. Instead, he gulped down his drink and signaled the waitress for another. "Okay, let's say you hire her. What's she going to do? Do you know if she even types?"

Ryan's brow went up an inch. "What difference would that make? She'd be out in the field—a fixer." He smiled. "Like you."

"Now I know you're crazy!" Jack pushed his plate away. He took a big breath. He was just getting started. "You give her a license to kill, and believe me, she'll kill, alright! She'll be a killing machine—*because she's driven to avenge Carl's death*. If you do this, you'll regret it."

"I disagree. In the first place, her kamikaze tendencies will always be in check because, despite her loss, unlike you, she still has a lot to live for—her kids."

Jack reeled back, as if Ryan had punched him. *Touché, boss.*

Instead he said, "There are other reasons, she'd be all wrong for wet work. Those kids have already lost one parent. Should something happen to her, who's going to look after them? Her crazy aunt?"

"During your investigation of Donna, what was your take on her?"

Jack felt his chest tighten. "In...in what regard?"

"I'm asking if you ever saw her have a meltdown."

"No."

"Did she throw tantrums? Was she depressed?"

"No. She was...sad, I guess is the right word."

"I can imagine why. It's got to be frustrating to lose the person you love most in the world, and not be able to do anything about it."

"Tell me about it," Jack muttered.

He kept his eyes on the waves. It was high tide. The waves rolled in all the way under the pylons that held the restaurant well above the surf and sand.

The way he felt at that very minute, if a wave cracked the glass at that moment and pulled Ryan out with it, Jack would do nothing to save him.

He wondered to himself: *Why should I? He's going to ruin the one reason I have for living.*

This deep emptiness was something Jack had not felt since he'd last seen Donna. Now it filled him again, like the specter of an unwanted friend. "Go ahead then, ask her." Jack leaned back in his chair. "My guess is that she'll take a pass."

"You're on. I'd bet a Benjamin on that." Ryan reached for a roll. "In the meantime, you'll head up her background investigation."

At first, Jack was going to protest. Then it struck him:

Great. That way I can ensure she doesn't get on with Acme.

In fact, it would be better all the way around. If Donna Stone were looking for revenge, she'd get herself into trouble with or without Acme's help.

Suddenly, Jack wasn't hungry. He drank his dinner instead.

13

Open-Source Intelligence

They know what you're thinking.

No, they are not clairvoyant. They read what you post online —on your blog, or on Facebook.

They can see you, too. You're so cute, especially when bathed in an Instagram glow!

Or maybe your thoughts are succinct enough for a mere one hundred and forty characters. If so, Tweet away.

Didn't you win a blue ribbon at the county fair? They read about it in the newspaper.

Did you know your cousin posted a video of you on YouTube? In it, you're blowing out the candles on your birthday cake. (FYI: They were somewhat concerned for you because you ran out of breath before you hit the last flame! Seems the years have indeed taken their toll.)

And every time you tap the GPS on your cell phone—to find a route or catch a bus—they are at the other end, waiting for you.

Yes, following you. Isn't that what you wanted?

They call it open-source intelligence, or OSINT.

You may prefer, "Big Brother is watching."
Either way, rest assured, they are everywhere.

THE FIRST TIME THE JET-BLACK BRUTALE 800 DRAGSTER DROVE up to the doorstep of Jack's Venice Beach apartment, it was so loud that he thought it was barreling through the front door.

The biker's helmet came off, revealing a woman—hell, make that girl, since she couldn't have been twenty-one yet —with jet-black spiked hair, darkly lined eyes, and four tiny nose rings in her right nostril. She wore a cropped T-shirt emblazoned, GOTTA WEAR A TAT TO GET U SOME OF THAT, with an arrow that pointed straight down.

Naturally Jack's eyes were drawn to where it stopped: at her slim waist, just above her low-riding black leather jeans.

On the other hand, her appraisal of him was no more than a cursory shrug. "Emma Honeycutt. Ryan sent me. I'm supposed to assist you with the investigation." She didn't wait for an invitation. She just waltzed past him, into the apartment.

Maybe Ryan isn't so serious about Donna's vetting after all, Jack thought.

But now, as he walked around the dining room table and perused the stacks of research waiting for him, he was dumbstruck by all she'd done in such a short period of time.

"Way to go, slick. But are you sure you got everything?" He was kidding, of course.

"Probably not. But at least it's better than what Acme had

on Mrs. Stone when I started this project." She pointed to a very slim file.

In fact, it was the file Jack had pulled together specifically on Donna during his investigation of Carl's death.

"Since there's wasn't much to begin with, I also took the liberty of combing through your files from the investigation into Carl's death," Emma continued.

"If I remember correctly," Jack said, "Acme's recruiting ops went in with a proctoscope before bringing him onboard as an operative."

"You're right. Needless to say, I was hoping to find the kind of intel that would give us some insight as to why Donna and Carl were attracted to each other in the first place. As husband and wife, Carl should have known her better than anyone. I'd hoped something—*anything*—in his files could give us more clarity on her. But for the most part, it was a wash." Emma tossed the file aside.

Jack nodded silently. No one knew that better than him. He'd made sure the file kept strictly to the facts. He hadn't wanted his obsession with her clouding his investigation into Carl's murder.

Emma had her head stuck in his fridge. When she resurfaced, she was holding a Pork Slap Pale Ale in each hand. She handed him one. "When I was done pulling all this dry stuff—it's a real snore, let me tell you—I started trolling for the good stuff—you know open-source intel—on both of them."

He popped open the beer and took a sip. "Considering our profession, I presume you drew a blank with Carl."

"You'd think so, right? Nah. The years BD—before Donna, that is—produced a gold mine of commentary from his old girlfriends"—she rolled her eyes—"all two hundred and thirteen of them. And those are just the ones I found on Facebook and a couple of online dating sites! You know, things like his pick-up lines, how long it took him to run the bases, his favorite positions . . ."

Suddenly, the thought of what might end up in his own file made him queasy. "You mean to tell me your research methodology is that thorough?"

"It's why I get paid the big bucks." She laughed. When he didn't join in, she muttered, "It's a joke. I'm an intern, remember?"

Jack took a big gulp. Ryan would be a fool not to hire this girl full-time, he thought. "So a bunch of old girlfriends are reminiscing about the best—or worst—lay they ever had. What does that have to do with tracking down the Quorum, let alone finding where he hid the intel they want so badly?"

"Who said anything about 'worst'?" she smirked knowingly. "And for that matter, who said they were all 'old' girlfriends?"

Jack shrugged. "He doted on his wife. But sometimes the job calls for a little…well, moonlighting."

"Is that what you call it, moonlighting? Ha! Okay yeah, sure, playing raven is all in a day's work. But this isn't about his 'moonlighting.' It's the key to why Carl and Donna fell in love, and why he decided she was Miss Right—especially for someone who was such a big player to begin with."

Jack had to concede she had a point. "Okay, so what's your take regarding his love life, BD?"

"He liked playing one side against the other. And he was into 'catch and release.' In other words, as soon as he scored, he moved onto the next challenge." Emma plopped down on the couch. "I presume he was the same way in the field—that is to say, somewhat competitive."

Jack winced. "Sure, I can vouch for that."

"Also, he took chances, and accepted the toughest assignments because they have the biggest rewards."

"Really? You got all that by reading the comments of his former lovers?"

"It was a quantitative analysis. All I had to do was count the number of *Kama Sutra* positions he was able to pull off and weigh them by how strenuous they are."

Seeing Jack's scowl, she sighed. "Just kidding! Seriously man, lighten up." The levity went out of her voice. "Jack, there's another thing you need to know about the Carls of the world. Because they're ego-driven, sometimes they get sloppy"—she paused in order to take a deep breath—"and for that matter, sometimes they can be turned."

"Look Emma, Carl may have been a player—and yes, he was an arrogant son of a bitch, too. But he was loyal to Acme and to his country. He proved that many times over."

She shrugged. "Just telling you like it is. Don't get your manties in a twist, okay?"

"I'm boxer briefs, in case you're wondering," he growled. "But I presume you've already pulled up my Visa account and scanned it for that kind of pertinent intel."

"Your last underwear purchase was at Nordstrom—two pair, Hugo Boss, Regular. Both black—"

"What the hell?"

"Just kidding! It was a lucky guess, I swear!" In order to hide her smirk, she went over and plucked an iPad from the desk. "I guess that's the ideal segue to Carl after Donna. I did find two things of interest, both having to do with her."

She swiped the screen until a video appeared. "He mentioned meeting her at a firing range near his apartment at the time. I searched within fifteen miles of his residence, and found the right one. As it turns out, the range keeps its webcam footage for a ten-year period."

From what Jack could tell, he was looking at an interior firing range. There were several shooters, all male except for a slim, pretty, long-haired brunette in jeans and a T-shirt. She couldn't have been more than twenty or twenty-one.

It was Donna.

She wore safety goggles and held her pistol two-fisted. The first few shots hit the target, but they weren't bull's-eyes. By the frown on her perfect cupid-bow mouth, she was obviously frustrated by this.

Jack then noticed the man just beyond her—Carl. Like Donna, he was around eight or nine years younger at the time. From the tilt of Carl's head and his sly grin, Jack could tell that his old friend was scoping her out.

Within minutes, Carl had introduced himself. In no time at all, he was giving her hands-on instruction on how to steady her aim.

"Cute meet, wasn't it? I guess you could call it 'love at first shot.'" Emma clicked onto another video box. "Now, here's a few days prior to their meeting, at the same range."

Not only the same range, but the same girl, too. This time, her aim was not only steady, it was a string of consistent bull's eyes, no matter what target was in front of her.

And right through the heart, especially if the target was of a sinister man.

Emma paused the video. "It was quite a ploy to get him

to notice her. And it worked like a charm. Maybe Ryan is right, and she's a natural for field ops."

Jack winced. "She'll have to be more than a good flirt." He wondered if Carl had ever found out how well she shot.

"Oh, I'll say she's that, and more, when it comes to Carl." She laughed. "I'll bet you can guess Donna's email password."

Jack shook his head. "I have no idea."

"Really? Go ahead and try." She waited patiently.

Jack thought a moment. "MaryJeffTrisha? Her date of birth? Their address? Don't leave me in suspense."

"It's 'Alex0417,' the combination of Carl's middle name and his birthday." Emma raised a brow. "Something tells me she'll be one toxic avenger."

Jack hated the thought that Emma was right.

Seeing what she pulled up on Carl, he was almost afraid to ask, but he had to: "What kind of OSINT have you found on Donna?"

"Apparently, she's not much for socializing—online, anyway. Ryan should appreciate that. I haven't found any accounts for her on Twitter, Pinterest, Instagram, or Face-book. I'll keep monitoring her internet activity for any social media log-ins." She swiped the screen again. Mary's face appeared. She was older now. "On the other hand, her eight-year-old, Mary, has a Facebook account." From what I can tell, Mom hasn't caught onto this fact yet. As for email, the Internet browser used by the family Stone isn't the most secure one out there." She rolled her eyes.

Wow, thought Jack, Mary is her mother in miniature—Donna 2.0! He wondered what Trisha looked like, now that she was no longer an infant.

Well, he'd soon find out.

Jack forced a smile onto his face. "All the same, let's see if the former Donna...what's her maiden name again?" He picked up Carl's personal information file. "Here it is— Donna Shives. Let's see if any other anomalies pop up in your research that might burst Ryan's bubble about her."

"You know, he wasn't always a fan." She slid a single sheet of paper his way. It was an Acme memorandum:

To: Carl Stone

Fr: Ryan Clancy

Re: Recent Change in Your Personal Status

It has come to my attention that you've recently married. First and foremost, let me congratulate you on your nuptials. At the same time, I presume you are well aware that Acme protocol mandates that the company be informed of any change in personal status—especially an issue as important as an engagement, let alone a marriage. Such information, provided in a timely fashion, helps alleviate any uncomfortable situations that may arise in light of the background check that will take place, according to Clause 14(a)(5) of your employment contract.

Again, my best wishes to you and your new bride.

Ryan

"Talk about cold." Jack frowned. "I guess Ryan wasn't a happy camper when he found out Carl dodged company protocol."

"Why would Carl do that?" Emma asked.

"Great question. I presume the former Miss Shives holds the answer."

She paused. "Have you met her?"

"Nope. And by the way things look, I never will, either. And neither will you. Ryan has given strict instructions that she's never to know about this investigation. He'll tell her after she agrees to join Acme."

Emma nodded. "I don't blame him for wanting it that way. It'll be easier for her to say yes if the vetting has already taken place. In the time since Carl's death, Ryan has gotten to know her pretty well, hasn't he?"

"I guess." Jack tipped his beer can at her. "Still, that doesn't mean she'll be his Femme Nikita."

Emma clinked his can with hers. "Something tells me if push comes to shove, she'll be able to take care of herself."

He shrugged. "Look, I'll bet you a pizza we'll dig up something that takes her out of the running."

Based on everything he'd already learned about Donna—including the stuff he left out of his final report on her husband's death—he knew it was wishful thinking on his part.

Here's hoping she won't sacrifice the life she has in order to avenge Carl's death, he thought.

"I'll take that bet, in a heartbeat. In fact"—Emma rummaged around the desk until she found a specific file, and handed it to him. "I've dug up a couple of very interesting items already. One is her second grade teacher's assessment. Another may or may not have anything to do with Donna. The person of interest is never positively identified, but considering the dates and locations, not to mention what we just saw on the video taken from the shooting range, I'm pretty sure it's her."

He looked down at the file, curious as to what it held.

"If we're ordering the pizza now, you'll have to front me the cash." Emma smiled. "I'm living on an intern's salary, remember?"

He sighed as he handed her a twenty.

As an afterthought, he added, "Anything but anchovies!" At the same time, she asked, "How do you feel about anchovies?"

In unison they countered, "Okay, half and half."

The harder decision—and one he'd have to make himself, was what to do if Donna turned out to be right for the job.

He'd do anything to protect her.

He'd even lie about her to Ryan.

He hoped it wouldn't come down to that.

From the look of the file Emma had handed him, he had a long night ahead.

[FROM THE STUDENT RECORD ARCHIVES OF THE PASADENA Country Day School, Mrs. Lawson's Second Grade Class Parent Correspondence Copy file:]

Dear Mrs. Shives,

A note of thanks for the basket of tasty blueberry muffins, delivered to me this morning by our sweet little student, Donna. I shared them with the other teachers and Principal Conklin, all of whom were very appreciative!

The note in the basket mentioned your apprehension that Donna isn't endearing herself to the other second grade students, especially the other girls.

Sadly, there may be some credence to your concerns.

If you remember, the decision to allow Donna to skip a grade was one taken with great caution on both your part and that of the school's. Her scores in both the Stanford-Benet and Wechsler Intelligence Scale tests were so impressive that holding her back would have been a grave discourtesy to her.

And while she lacks the social maturity that comes when a child's beginning grade in school is the first as opposed to the second grade, Donna is certainly an "old soul." Personally, I dislike this overused term. But in this case, I feel it is apropos.

Donna is indeed wise beyond her years.

She may not be as old as the others in the class, but she certainly takes on the role of "big sister" with some of the meeker children in the class. Unfortunately, her naturally sweet demeanor and strident sense of right and wrong have put her at odds with some of the more dominant children in the class.

Cases in point: One of our volunteer playground mommies was privy to an interaction between your daughter and some of the other second-grade girls, who don't have her inclusive sensibilities. During one of the girls' less thoughtful acts towards a shy little boy, this mommy likened Donna's somewhat colorful chastisement of the clique to that of a "sailor on a drunken binge."

In a second incident later that week, after this particular second-grade girls' clique had cordoned off a section of the playground as their private domain, one of our student teachers watched as Donna coerced them into the janitorial shed and threatened to leave them in there to starve unless they allowed some of the other girls to play with them.

Rest assured, the girls were released from captivity by the end of the play period.

The complexity of the trap she set was certainly impressive (according to the report she dressed it up as a "Disney castle"), and would make any Cubbette scoutmaster proud. (I understand you head up the neighborhood troop for that age group). And frankly, I was more concerned when I heard the girls were drawing straws to determine which of them was to be eaten first, should it come to that.

Still, in light of these incidents, I think it's fair to say that Donna's skills at conflict resolution are certainly in need of fine-tuning.

That being said, I hope you can work with me in encouraging her to curtail her candid remarks and more strident actions during times of confrontation.

Yours truly,

Mrs. Lunsford, Lead Teacher - Second Grade

FROM THE LOS ANGELES POLICE DEPARTMENT'S VIDEO *transcript of the confession of Boyd Rutherford McGinnis, a.k.a. the Lover's Lane Executioner:*

McGinnis:

...and then I made him eat the barrel of my Beretta. His brains spattered all over the girl. That's okay. I made his last few minutes on Earth pretty darn memorable, what with the way I rode that little lass—right there in front of him. "At least one of us got to break her cherry," is what I told him. Turns out she really wasn't a virgin, but he didn't need to know that.

Detective Concha:

That would be the Dempsey girl, right?

McGinnis:

Yep. Little Debbie Snack Cakes is what I called her. *Whooeee!* How she loved them things! Was a two-fisted eater, too! Disgusting, like she was raised in a barn. Pretty damn funny considering where I buried her. She had enough meat on her bones that I kept her around for—let's see now, six months? Maybe seven. She was a beggar, that one. That's exactly what you want in a pet, isn't it? She would do anything to stay alive, if you catch my drift? Well, at least it kept me off the streets for a while. You boys must have felt like you were on vacation.

Detective Concha:

Not exactly. Scum like you always resurfaces, somewhere, somehow. You know what they say, 'Shit floats to the top.' So, what you've just said would account for the gap between November and May of that year. But it wasn't the longest time between killings. Of course, what we didn't know at the time was you had been permanently retired. In fact, it's been over thirteen, maybe fourteen years...Boyd? Jeez, guy! You look like you've seen a ghost.

McGinnis:

I...Yeah, okay, actually there was an incident that made me

reconsider my 'legacy,' if you will. Now that the doctors say I'm a goner anyhow, I guess if the world is going to know about everything—which, from what you've recorded already, you can see how you boys were pretty sloppy, picking up the pieces and all—

Detective Concha:

Trust me, Boyd. I only wish we'd caught you in the act. We would have put you out of your misery, and some of those poor kids would still be around today. So what happened? Did you get hit on that psychopathic head of yours and finally come to your senses? Or did the heavens open up and an angel descended, giving you salvation?

McGinnis:

Hell, no, wasn't any angel! It was...it was...a *she-devil*! [Sobbing]...

Detective Concha:

Geez, Boyd, get a hold of yourself! Here, take a swig of your Coke.

[Silence...Gulping. A loud burp.]

McGinnis:

You're right. The last killings were the Jamison boy and that big-titted girlfriend of his—the one with the red panties. Of course, you wouldn't know what color they were, since I took them with me—as a souvenir. That one was a wildcat! Fought the whole time I was up inside of her. I saw right off that she would have made a lousy pet. Nothing else I could do but put a bullet in her head afterward. But then, I was so pissed at myself for losing the chance to take someone home with me that I broke my own rule—you know, at least six weeks between hunts—that I went out the very next week. It happened up in Laurel Canyon, on a dead-end street where a builder had a couple of spec houses with a great view of the whole city. But he must have gone bust or something, because the houses were never completed. The high school kids used to go up there and feel each other up. I thought it might be a great place to pick off a few, but…well, things didn't go as I'd planned.

Detective Concha:

What do you mean?

McGinnis:

Usually I'd wait until they were down to their underwear, but this girl wasn't having any of the boy's shenanigans. She'd just slap his hands away, like some sort of prude. Hell, I don't think he got as far as second base. Fine by me. If she were a virgin, I'd rather break her in myself. Besides, them kind of girls make the best pets. So I smacked the gun against the window. That scared the Bejesus out of them—well, the boy anyway. He was wetting himself even before he got out of the car. But not her. She just sat there, staring at me, as bold as you please. I yelled at her to come out, but she shrugged. So I slapped the cuffs on him, and then I took the gun and stuck it in his mouth, just to show her that I meant business. That usually had the girls begging and pleading. They'd rather give it up than watch the poor boys' brains get spattered all over the place.

Detective Concha:

Yeah, I guess they figure it will give them a reputation as a cold-hearted bitch or something.

McGinnis:

I wouldn't know myself, since I was always an outcast in high school. I would have taken any pussy that came my way, even from a mean girl.

Detective Concha:

For some reason, that doesn't surprise me. So, then what happened?

McGinnis:

I wanted the boy to watch, but the idiot passed out. The girl, though, she was something else! She said, "Don't mind him. We don't need an audience. Come and get it." Just like that, as if we were playing a game or something! No one had ever done that to me before—you know, come on to me. She smiled at me and waved me over, as if she'd been waiting for me all her life...Hey, that look on your face right now can't be any more surprised than what I felt.

Detective Concha:

I doubt that. What did you do then?

McGinnis:

What the hell do you think? Of course, I went over to her. Before I could say anything, she came up real close, and started unbuckling my belt. I was so surprised that I just...I just stood there. "Thank God there's finally a real man in my life," she said. "I'm tired of all those little boys." Then she's pulling down my zipper, real slow and sexy like. Not at all scared like the others. As if she's enjoying it...and I was, too. "Wow," she said, "You're so big!" No one had ever called me that. So I look down for just a second. The next thing I know, she's slammed my hand against the car, and the gun goes flying. Then her knee comes up, popping me in the groin. When I buckled over, she punched me in the Adam's apple. While I was gasping for air and down for the count, she saunters over to where the gun was, picks it up, and aims for my genitals. "Someone should neuter you," she tells me. "I guess I'm elected." I'm still doubled over in pain, and scared shitless. "This is going to hurt," she says. "And there will be a lot of pain and blood. You won't die, but you'll live the rest of your life knowing you can't hurt another human being. At least, not with that itty-bitty thing of yours."

[Sound of suspect sobbing.]

When she did it, I must have passed out. But those kids must have called it in because I woke up in a hospital bed. The nurse said I must have tried to kill myself, and that they'd confiscated my gun. I'm ruined down there. But the girl was right. I never hurt anyone, ever again.

Detective Concha:

Wow. I've been on the force for thirty-three years, and I've never heard something like this. You wouldn't happen to know her name, would you?

McGinnis:

It's burned into my brain. When the boy was yanked out of the car, he called her 'Donna.'

Detective Concha:

If she was, what, fifteen or sixteen then, that would make her around thirty now. Ha! Well, what do you know!

McGinnis:

I'll tell you what I know! Now that I'm going to see my Maker, I pray I'll never meet her again—either on this earth, or in the Hell that's waiting for me in the great beyond. Every time I hear that name—Donna—I get chills up my spine.

Detective Concha:

Donna. *Donna, Donna, Donna.*

[Sound of Suspect, sobbing.]

Detective Concha to Prison Guard:

I got what I need. Get him the hell out of here.

14

Naked

A spy acting without a cover, or backup, is said to be naked.

A person not wearing clothes is said to be naked.

A spy who has no cover, and doesn't bother to cover up, is looking for all sorts of trouble, and will probably find it.

JACK WAS GLAD THAT RYAN HAD KEPT HIS PROMISE TO HIM—TO have an asset on twenty-four hour surveillance in the house Acme rented across from the Stone residence.

"In fact, since you're charged with Donna's vetting, you should move back in," Ryan suggested.

"That would make things easier," Jack acknowledged. "I won't be cramping the surveillance op's style, will I?"

Ryan roared with laughter at the question, to the point that he teared up. Finally, after he collected himself, he sputtered, "Trust me, not in a million years. With the schedule you'll both be keeping, you'll barely run into each other."

Jack wasn't sure, but he could have sworn Ryan added, under his breath, *If you know what's good for you.*

"Did…did you say something?" Jack asked.

Ryan looked up, surprised. "Me? No!" He dismissed Jack with a wave of his hand.

He heard Ryan laughing again as he closed the door.

The place hadn't changed much since he'd taken up residence there last, except for the fact that the once-beige clapboard siding was now painted a bright canary yellow. The Acme asset living there must have had a green thumb. A riot of pink tea roses now draped the white picket fence that circled the yard.

As in most covert-ops organizations, Acme's operatives and assets came in all ages, shapes, and sizes. Since Acme didn't know if and when the Quorum would come knocking on Donna's door, this agent's long-term mission was to keep watch over the Stones until it was determined that they were out of danger, and to be their first line of defense in case trouble did come calling.

Although Jack's host would be expecting him, there was to be a code word used, to ascertain he was the legitimate shadow: "I'm here to clean your pipes."

The garage was to be left open, so that he could park his vehicle—in this case, a white cargo van marked *Perfect Plumbing.* As per his instructions, he shut the rolling garage door afterward, so that no one could see a second car from the street. Then he grabbed his duffel bag and walked around to the back, so that he couldn't be observed by anyone else as he entered.

Like all the backyards in Hilldale, the one for this home

was expansive. In fact, it was large enough for a pool and an outdoor terrace.

So, this is what it's like to score a babysitting mission, thought Jack. Sweet set-up, and on Acme's dime, no less. Maybe I should consider something like this for my dotage —that is, if I don't go out, guns blazing.

All Jack was told about his host was to expect a single female. He presumed she was middle-aged, and one of those quiet types you never gave a second glance, since her mission called for her to be a nondescript, unobtrusive neighbor and keep to herself.

As per his instructions, he knocked on the back door.

And waited.

Then waited some more.

He noticed a buzzer to his right and rang it. Then he rang it again.

Maybe she was older than he was led to believe. Had she forgotten to put in her hearing aid? He envisioned the elderly woman in some commercial he'd seen during one of his agonizingly long waits in some airport terminal. She'd fallen, and her feeble shouts, "Help me, I can't get up..." weren't heard by anyone, aptly bringing home the message that the purchase of an emergency alert bracelet was inevitable.

Jack was struck with the vision of having to help some old lady in and out of her Barcalounger when he should be making his case as to why Donna should never put herself in danger.

Hell, this is my nightmare, he thought.

Just then the door opened.

The blonde standing in front of him was tall enough that she didn't have to be wearing the five-inch pink stilettos strapped to her feet, and certainly too young, and too drop-dead gorgeous to be living on some cul-de-sac in suburbia.

And she was definitely too naked to be answering the door to a stranger's knock on her back door.

Granted, she was in the process of draping herself in a sheer gauzy pink robe, but it did nothing to cover up her perfectly sculpted curves, let alone her very large breasts, which at eye level seemed to defy gravity like twin zeppelins flying side by side.

To break the spell they cast on him, she snapped her fingers in front of his eyes. "Hey, up here."

Jack blinked, then murmured, "Um...I'm here to clean your pipes."

Her eyes narrowed as she gave him the once-over. Finally, she smiled. "I like a man with a plan. Come on in."

As he followed her in, he thought, I owe Ryan big time for this assignment.

She didn't stop until they reached the living room, which was painted indigo blue and held a semicircular-tufted white leather couch that faced the window overlooking the pool. One wall was devoted to a mirrored wet bar with rows of liquors rivaling any he'd seen in the world's best hotels.

As she bent over to pick up a martini glass from the coffee table, her robe rose just enough for a peek-a-boo view of what lay beneath. This time, before she was upright and had turned around toward him, he'd forced his eyes out the window, toward the glare of the undulating pool. She tilted her head to one side. "Coffee? Tea? Or maybe..." She let this tantalizing proposal linger in the air long enough that it atomized any variety of fantasies, then added "a martini?"

Jack cleared his throat. "Scotch. Thanks." He hesitated, then held out his hand. "I'm Jack Craig."

She shook it. "Yes, I know. Your reputation precedes you." She headed to the other side of the bar. Scanning the shelves, she saw what she was looking for—a bottle of Glenlivit XXV. She poured a full tumbler of it and handed it to him. "Nola Janoff."

Your reputation precedes you, too, he thought. No wonder Ryan conveniently forgot to mention who'd be hosting me.

He tried to remember the last he'd heard about Acme's infamous honeypot.

As if reading his mind, Nola murmured, "It was the Rio incident." She shrugged.

"Yeah, right, a few months back." Jack nodded. "There was something about you getting the goods on Juan Domingo Cámpora, the head of Argentina's covert-op agency, *Central de Reunión de Inteligencia Militar*. Wasn't there also some scandal involving our client—his boss in the *Secretaría de Inteligencia?*"

Nola sighed. "José Félix Vidal. Dreamy blue eyes. He claimed he inherited them from his great-grandfather, Joseph Mengele. Considering his bedside manner, I could believe it." She downed her martini, then poured another out of the shaker. "Turns out both men were selling Argentina's state secrets to the Venezuelans. They had other things in common as well—a love for fine French wines, Cuban cigars, their country's thoroughbred racehorses—not to mention a passion for sex acts requiring the skills of a contortionist."

"I heard you almost didn't make it out. So, here's to the fickle finger of fate." He tapped his glass with hers.

"Yes, well, Acme passed along my intel to the Argentinean president, via POTUS. Scored a few brownie points for the home team, right?" She shrugged. "But my boy toys weren't so happy to find out I'd squealed on them. Too bad. That's what happens when you trust a pretty face." She batted her eyes in mock innocence. "Yeah, it was a tight situation, but I escaped thanks to a very handsome ship's purser on a Crystal Cruise Line ship. Ever wonder why so many cruisers fall overboard? I can tell you firsthand. It's a little game called 'Walk the Plank," which is played with a bottle of tequila, an eye patch, and something that should be as long as a cutlass, but always comes up short, if you catch my drift." She batted her eyes. "You'd think Ryan would have merited that as worthy enough for a little vacation. No such luck. I guess it's why I'm stuck out here in suburgatory, babysitting the widow Stone"—she plucked the toothpick holding an olive out of her glass, and sucked on it—"with you, of all people. So, what's your story? I presume Pope Ryan also assigned you to this mission as some sort of penance. Am I right?"

"I guess you could say that." Jack winced at the thought. "Her husband, Carl, was blown sky high, and it may have been because of something he was couriering for me to Ryan. The item in question is still missing. From the chatter Acme has picked up, we have some reason to believe it didn't disintegrate with him."

She frowned. "Good old Carl. May he rest in peace." Her

prayer gave her another excuse to make a toast—and down her drink accordingly.

"So, you knew him?"

She snickered. "Not in the Biblical sense, no. Only by reputation—and from what I hear, I missed out on something...*big*." She laughed as she held her hands almost a foot apart. "The way he went at it, he was sure to get someone mad at him—if not another shooter or some pissed off dictator, then a jealous mistress or a pissed-off husband."

Jack turned toward the other side of the room, where the picture window faced the Stone residence. "So much for an untarnished legacy."

"Hey, I'm no saint either, and I'll admit it. It's probably why this job is cut out for me." She slid onto a barstool. "On the other hand, you're a regular knight in shining armor. The wife must be quite a lady."

"She is...was." He frowned. "We're no longer an item. My job—it got to her, too." Time to change the topic, he thought. "I've been away from this particular surveillance gig for a year. What can you tell me about her? Any patterns?"

"What, with three kids? You better believe it. She walks the two oldest children to the elementary school. Afterward, she takes baby Trisha with her to the grocery store—usually on Mondays and Fridays, depending on whether she hits Target, too. The eldest, Mary, now eight, has a couple of after-school activities—ballet on Tuesdays, and gymnastics on Thursdays. Jeff is in first grade. For him there's little league and soccer practice—on Wednesdays and Fridays, respectively. His games are on Saturdays or Sundays. If there's a dental or doctor's appointment, unless it's an emergency, she schedules them for Mondays. Otherwise any sort of shopping involving the children takes place on that day, too. I've also got the elementary school calendar, so that I know what days or evenings she may leave the house for a school function. The kids are fed, bathed, and in bed by eight o'clock. She watches very little television. Mostly, she reads, or bakes—homemade breads, sometimes pies or cakes. And like clockwork, she gets on the treadmill, for at least an hour, sometimes longer. But when she can get a babysitter— usually her Aunt Phyllis—she'll go for a nice long jog. Or to the firing range. And by the way, she's a pretty decent shot."

"Yes, I seem to remember that." Jack smiled when he heard Phyllis's name. She'd certainly be on his call sheet this time around.

"In fact," Nola continued, "Phyllis is coming on Saturday, so she'll probably take a run then."

"You seem to have her schedule down pat. Have you noticed anyone snooping around the house when she takes off?"

"No, not once."

He was relieved about that. He still felt guilty about having pulled up stakes. "Nola, have you struck up a friendship?"

She shrugged. "I guess you can call it that. I go out of my way to be friendly, but because I don't have kids, I'm not naturally in her fly zone. But I borrow a lot—you know, sugar, hedge clippers—anything to get her talking. In fact, this ice bucket is hers." She pointed to the cut glass crystal ice bucket sitting on the counter. "From what I've observed, she pretty much keeps to herself, except when her kids have play dates—which are a lot." She rolled her eyes.

"Have any of the other women tried to cozy up to her?"

"Yes—and she's polite, but I notice that if she's invited to a gathering that doesn't involve the children—you know, like a parents' night out, or a neighborhood cocktail party—she'll have some excuse to pass. She doesn't want to field questions all night about a husband who doesn't exist." She shook her head in awe. "Donna is certainly keeping up her end of the bargain with Ryan. Still, the fact that she's married to the Invisible Man makes some of these women nervous. I can handle it, but truthfully, Jack, suburbia is not easy on single women—which is what they consider her around here."

"But they know she's married."

Nola raised a brow. "In name only. From what they see for themselves, he's always on extended business trips, or he's just left on last night's red eye, or somehow they've just missed him." She shook her head. "It doesn't help that she's also quite a looker—or haven't you noticed?"

Jack could feel his face heating up.

Nola laughed. "Don't worry. I wouldn't expect the celebrated Jack Craig to be a eunuch."

"I'm not Carl Stone, if that's what you're implying."

"Not at all—and thank goodness for that. The last thing the world needs is another one of him—God rest his soul." Her lips curled into a brittle smile. "Although I'm sure the grieving Mrs. Stone would disagree. Even if Carl hadn't been a spy, he would have fit right in. Too many of the men around these parts have wandering eyes, and hands. I speak from personal experience—" She stopped short. Her mouth dropped open. "Aw, hell, I forgot! Speaking of which, you'll have to excuse me. I've got to make a quick call, to one of the neighborhood Lotharios. Otherwise, he'll be knocking on my back door any moment now."

"You mean—right *now*?"

"Yes, silly!...Oh my goodness! Did you think I always walk around like this? Or that maybe I put this on—for *you*?" That set her off into peals of laughter. "Frankly, I wasn't expecting you until tomorrow."

Jack frowned. "I take it, then, you don't believe in keeping a low profile."

"If I did, you wouldn't have half the intel I just gave you. Believe me, the men here gossip as much as their wives— and they find the demure Mrs. Stone quite intriguing." She pointed upstairs. "Choose any one of the bedrooms you want—except for the master, in the back." Her eyes swept over him. "Because believe me, if you do, you won't get much sleep."

He heard her loud and clear.

He chose the front bedroom that gave him the best view of Donna's house.

He missed her.

He couldn't wait to get that very first glimpse of her again.

He didn't have to wait long. He had just tossed his bag on the bed when the shades opened in one of the second-story windows of Donna Stone's house—the room belonging to Trisha.

Donna stood in the window.

She looked exactly as he remembered her.

Today, she wore a tank top and shorts. In one hand she held a retractable measuring tape. She lifted her hands to the top of the windowsill, then side by side within the sash. This movement propelled her chest forward. As she eyed the measurement, she mouthed it to herself.

He was mesmerized.

He missed her voice.

He missed watching the way her body moved.

Just as she lowered the measuring tape on one side in order to measure the height of the sill, something outside the window caught her eye.

Oh hell, she saw me, he thought. Immediately he ducked below his window.

She smiled and laughed—not at him, though, but at Mary, who had driven up to the house on her bike and was waving to her mother.

Jack laughed, too—at himself for forgetting that the windows were tinted in such a way that no one could see inside the Acme rental.

His smile faded when he remembered why he was there.

He pulled out his iPad and scrolled the PDFs of all the intel Emma had gathered on Donna to date, until he found Aunt Phyllis's address, out in Pasadena.

Time to take a little trip to the other side of LA.

On his way to the stairwell, he passed the master suite. The door was closed. He was about to rap on it when he heard a duet of moans. Apparently, whomever she had in there with her hadn't taken no for an answer.

The longer he stood there, the louder they got. Finally, he got tired of waiting for a break in the action.

From what he'd just heard, she was in for the night anyway.

Instead, he scribbled a note in code words that let her know where he was going, and not to wait up for him. He stuck it on the fridge with the only magnet already there: it was glazed with a picture of a pert blonde, circa nineteen-fifties. She held a bow and arrow in her hands. The slogan on the magnet said:

Stupid Cupid! I'll Get My Own Damn Man!

He chuckled as he went out the door.

15

Pocket Litter

Like most things, authenticity is in the details. A spy in hostile territory knows this firsthand. In order to alter your true identity, it's smart to litter your pockets with the sort of items that help your cover.

For example, if you're pretending to be a sports fan on the way to a game, wear a fan jersey or hat, casual pants, and put real game tickets in your front pocket. If you're supposed to be on a business trip, put an airline ticket in your pocket made out in your alias, as well as business cards.

If you're parading around as a Congressperson, wear a red or blue tie, an American flag pin, and stuff your pockets with plenty of cash.

"YOU'RE NOT JUST YANKING MY LEG, ARE YOU, YOUNG MAN? You mean to tell me someone left my poor deceased brother-in-law, Dave Shives, an inheritance?" Phyllis looked up from the rose bush she was pruning.

"Perhaps. You see we're trying to determine if in fact he is the right David Shives." Jack winced. His fake glasses were giving him a headache. He had perfect eyesight, but because he couldn't find plain-glass frames, he had to settle for the lowest prescription cheaters he could find from the local drug store. As part of his disguise, he had tinted his hair with a gray rinse, and combed it all the way back in order to look older. An ill-fitting suit, skinny tie, tasseled loafers, suitcase, and a phony business card from a made-up company finished off his "insurance agent" look. "Apparently the man—the Mr. Shives we're looking for, and the benefactor—were in the same Army battalion unit during the Vietnam War. In fact, Mr. Shives saved the benefactor's life—something about enemy forces attacking, getting caught in a crossfire—"

"Huh?" She took off her sunglasses and squinted up at him. "He spent the whole time at the Presidio, in San Francisco. He was the cemetery NCO. You know, sort of like a grave digger and gardener, but fancier."

"Um...I think it was during his training—war games and the like." He ignored her stare. "Um...Anyway, Mr. Shives pulled his benefactor to safety, although the benefactor did suffer an injury. When they got home, they parted ways and lost touch. The benefactor never had a family—"

"Oh! You mean"—she pointed to his groin —"down there."

"Um...yes, that sounds about right." He pretended to find the fact on his clipboard. "Bottom line is this: In order to determine if in fact he is the right guy, I need you to answer a few questions, maybe dig out a few items that verify—"

"Whoa, wait up, young man." She dusted the dirt off her gardening gloves. "Just how much money has this Mr. Benefactor person bequeathed to Dave?"

"His name isn't 'Benefactor.' I have to say that because I have strict instructions not to divulge the name until I'm sure—"

"Okay, I read you loud and clear." She shook her head. "You know, Dave died almost ten years ago. His wife—my sister, Mary—predeceased him a decade before that. Poor thing. Breast cancer took her." She shrugged. "His illness was man-made." She pantomimed drinking from a bottle. "I came to live with Dave to help him raise his little girl, Donna."

"It doesn't matter that he passed. His heir—Donna, that is—will inherit the money in his place."

She nodded, relieved. "Good to know! Donna's got three kids, and no husband."

"Um…what?" He slid the glasses down the bridge of his nose so that he could see her clearly. Had Donna divulged to her aunt the truth of Carl's death?

"It's the truth—although the poor thing won't admit it." She leaned in and whispered, "She tells everyone he's traveling all the time, but that's a bunch of hooey! Carl Stone—to be honest, he was an odd duck anyway—took off and left her high and dry. Probably for some little chippie. He always did have a wandering eye." She arched a brow. "The children are devastated. They just want the truth, one way or the other. I told them myself, just the other day. Well, you can imagine her reaction. She hit the roof! Told me I had no right to make them think poorly of their daddy." She sighed and brushed away a tear with her gloved hand. "How much did you say the inheritance was again?"

"I didn't. Not yet, anyway, until we make sure we've got the right woman…I mean, man." He graced her with an innocent smile. "But while we're on the subject of your niece, tell me: is she an easygoing sort of girl?"

"If by that you mean, 'Is she a slut,' I can tell you upfront and center that there was none of that Coyote Ugliness in her, no 'Girls Gone Wild.' She grew up a sweet young lady— although she did have her fair share of boyfriends." She raised a brow. "People always want what they can't have, if you catch my drift."

"You mean, she was quite a flirt."

"I mean, she was—is—charismatic as all get-out. She wears her wedding band with pride, and the men still buzz around."

"I see." Even as Jack's heart was sinking, he tried to keep the smile on his face.

"No you don't. You think I'm saying she's a pushover. Far from it! She's just staying true blue to Carl." Her eyes narrowed as she scrutinized Jack. "I noticed you're not wearing a ring. If you want, I could put in a good word for you."

"No, I…I mean, no I'm not in a relationship right now—"

"That works to your favor, young man. Especially now that she may be coming into a little money." Phyllis leered knowingly at him. "And you're not exactly hard on the eyes, either. In fact, if you got yourself a pair of contacts and went to a better barber, you'd be fighting 'em off with a stick." She sighed. "In hindsight, it would be a lost cause. She really does believe in happily ever after. Carl Stone is a dang fool. She'd do anything for him."

She'd do anything for Carl.

Would she even work for Acme as a way to avenge his death?

Jack knew what that would entail. Nola was a perfect example of it.

So was Tatyana Zakharov.

It was the last thing Jack would wish for any woman.

He had to find some reason to convince Ryan that his scheme wouldn't work.

He put his hand on Phyllis' shoulder. "Perhaps you have some mementos that can help make the case that we have the right man."

"I'll tell you what, there's a box in the garage—top shelf, marked 'Shives.' Big bold letters. When Donna came home from the hospital with her last little one, I stayed with her for a while. Donna tossed out a lot of stuff she just didn't want anymore—family photos and old letters, that sort of thing. She said it made her sad. I'm holding onto it anyway, in case the little ones get curious about their mama's folks. Heck, Carl had no family to speak of, so that makes me a living history lesson. Feel free to dig around in there. Just be sure to return it when you're done making your case, okay?"

She waved him off to go back to her pruning.

He found the box, no problem, and put it beside him on the car's passenger seat. He'd take it to Emma, back at the Venice apartment, which she used as her office, now that he was working from Hilldale. He could have her meet him, at Nola's, but he guessed she'd feel just as uncomfortable as he did with Nola's extracurricular activities.

Periodically, on the drive back to Hilldale, his eyes shifted toward the box. It bothered him that the items, which memorialized the average person, could be reduced to a sixteen-inch-by-twelve-inch-by-twelve-inch-square corrugated box.

For spies, it was even less. Nothing personal, no mementoes from their past, a mostly undocumented, unremembered life.

Perhaps the guns they left behind—that is, if they were not government-issued.

In most cases, even their IDs were false.

"ARE YOU INTERESTED IN DONNA'S RECIPE BOOK?" Emma asked.

Jack thought for a few moments, then shook his head. "I'm guessing there is nothing in it that can shed light on her character—unless she's entering a county fair cooking contest."

Emma nodded as she tossed the book to one side. "Hey, did you see this?" Emma held up a small pink leather book. Its pages were clasped in the middle with a band. "It's Donna's diary."

He held up his hand. "Now, that's what I'm talking about. Toss it over."

"I don't know if I should. It's pretty old. The binding may give way."

He walked over to retrieve it. It took just a second to pick the tiny lock, even without a key.

It was in Donna's handwriting, alright. The first passage

dated to her tenth birthday. The last was around the time she dated Carl.

Good, he thought. At least we'll get some sort of idea if she had an inkling of how serious Carl's job was. Maybe even some ideas of his actions, or moods.

He opened it and started reading.

THE PASSAGES WRITTEN WHEN SHE WAS TEN WERE ALL SUNSHINE and lollipops.

By the time she was eleven, the tone of her musings were darker—she'd figured out her mother was sick, although neither Dave nor Mary Shives spoke of her mother's illness to her.

She wasn't too popular in school to begin with. Her anxiety made her less so. One pal stuck it out with her—an older girl, named CeeCee. She was popular, and took Donna under her wing, like a big sister.

At first, anyway. Somewhere along the line, the relationship went south. In the diary, Donna didn't elaborate. But the heartache was there on the pages, both in prose and poetry.

Perhaps it had to do with the girl's boyfriend, a boy named Bobby. Jack could read between the lines: although the boy was several years older than Donna, she had a deep, schoolgirl crush on him.

Whereas Donna knew it would go nowhere, CeeCee must have felt otherwise. The telltale signs were her taunts toward Bobby at Donna's expense.

At that point, Donna wrote, *Why does CeeCee hate me so much? Does she suspect how I feel about him?*

One passage in particular was particularly poignant: about a tender kiss she'd shared with Bobby.

And CeeCee's reaction to it: heartless.

Cruel.

Jack did an Interpol data base search for CeeCee Connelly.

When he found her, he let out a low whistle.

"What gives?" Emma asked.

"I just found a couple of credible sources who may be able to give us some relatable insights on Donna. The husband is a top investor in the tech world, and the wife—"

Emma snorted. "What, Aunt Phyllis' farfetched memories aren't good enough for you?"

Jack held up a finger to shush her. He was already punching in the number he needed.

"Hi...yes, is this Bobby?...Oh, *Bob.* Yes, well, my name is Jack Craig. I'm with Acme Industries, and I'm calling in regard to a background check on a potential employee. You would have known her from her maiden name—Donna Shives. Your wife would have known her as well...Oh? Yes, of course it's not necessary to speak to her, too. I can imagine you both have very busy schedules. Your insights will be sufficient...Yes, I understand you knew Miss Shives—Donna —over two decades ago. Still, as a government-sanctioned agency, you can imagine our background checks have to be very thorough...Yes, I see. So you'd describe her as 'honest'...and a straight shooter...Ha! Yes, I know, no pun intended...an honest and heartfelt individual...the bravest person you've ever known? Wow, that's very high praise, sir...I'll be sure it all gets in the report. Yes, she's doing well —three children, still living in California...Tell her what? That you 'have always thought the best of her?' Um...I'm sorry Bob, in my capacity I won't be talking to Donna directly...Good, I'm glad you understand...Yes, thank you for your time and help. Good-bye."

Jack clicked off the line and sat quietly.

"Something wrong?" Emma asked.

He snapped to attention. "No, I guess not. The way that guy described Donna, I could tell he...he cared for her. And he certainly didn't want me talking to his wife. Sounds like there was some bad blood there."

Her eyes narrowed. "That makes Donna 'the one that got away.' With first boyfriends, those flames never grow cold. It's the essence of arrested development."

"Is that so? Has your first boyfriend sought you out?"

She smiled. "They *all* seek me out. I'm unforgettable."

Obviously, so is Donna, he thought. I can vouch for that.

16

Passive Probe

A mission in which an operative passively observes and records details about a target, location, or organization is called a passive probe.

If a date offers to passively probe you, allow him to do so at your own risk. Fair warning: nine months later, you may find yourself with a new mission.

"I HEARD FROM RYAN THIS MORNING." NOLA DIDN'T LOOK UP as she buttered her toast. "Crack of dawn. Ugh. You'd think the man would know better. I'm a working girl, after all."

Jack frowned. "Let me guess—he's checking up on my progress."

"That wasn't exactly how he put it." She put down her knife and met his eyes. "I would use the word 'non-progress,' if it existed. To be quite frank with you, his exact words were, 'Why in the hell is he dragging his fucking feet?' At that point I reminded him he was talking to a lady with delicate sensibilities—"

"Sweetheart, you curse like a sailor."

"Only while in the throes of passion, darling." She honored him with a sly smile. "So, how in the hell would you know?"

"The walls in this joint are paper thin," he muttered.

"Next time I'm out and about, I'll pick up a pair of earplugs for you." She hesitated. "Seriously, Jack, what's taking so long? Emma says she checks out fine on paper. Other than Hilldale's Stepford Wives, you can't find anyone who speaks ill of her—and only because she out-über-mommies them at every turn do they dislike her. To top it off, the woman runs mini-marathons for fun! And as much of a martyr as she is about the dearly-departed Carl, I'd say Donna Stone is ripe for the picking."

"That's the whole point." He rose from the table, exasperated. "If she says yes to Ryan, her reason better be rock solid! If it's revenge-driven, she may be more of a wild card than he would want. She'll put others' lives at risk, the way I put Carl's on the line. And with three kids—his three kids, I might add—she's got too much to lose." Seeing the doubt on her face, he threw up his hands in disgust. "Why am I the only one who sees this?"

"Because you're the only one in love with her."

Jack nodded. It felt good to admit it.

"Look, I need you to do me a favor," he muttered.

Curious, she tilted her head to one side. "Only if it's fun."

"I guess it could be, in the right light. Ask her to go out with you."

She sighed. "Hey, I know there are a lot of rumors flying around about me, but seriously, I don't swing that way—"

"No, not…! Hey, if anyone would know that, it's me, okay? What I mean is a girl's night out. Just the two of you. I'm sure her aunt would be happy to babysit. Tell her—I don't know, tell her you need a shoulder to cry on, then take her to a nice, quiet bar. Get a few drinks in her, to loosen her tongue. If you let your hair down, she might, too."

"What's the point, Jack?"

"I want to hear from her, how she feels—about him. I'm tired of trying to figure it out with second-hand intel. I want to…I want to hear it from her."

"In other words, you'll mike me."

"Yes. In fact, I'll take a seat where I can see her." And not just because he missed her, or that this would be a chance to see her, up close and personal.

He wanted to be there to see her face when she opened up.

Nola nodded. "Sure, okay, I'll try it. But don't get your hopes up. In all likelihood, she'll say no."

"It doesn't hurt to ask."

Nola tossed on a jacket over her negligee and started out the front door.

Jack sighed. "Whoa, hey—aren't you forgetting something?"

"Oh! You're right!" Nola turned around and ran upstairs.

A moment later when she came down, she had on stilettoes.

She's hopeless, he thought, as she headed out the door.

～

"DONNA SAID YES, SHE WOULDN'T MIND GOING OUT 'WITH A friend,' was how she put it," Nola added.

Jack knew Nola would never admit it, but she was touched that Donna put it that way.

By the looks of it, the place Nola chose for them was everything Jack had asked for: the lounge had a well-stocked bar. It was large, but intimate, with lots of nooks and crannies. There were mirrors everywhere, so that even in the lounge's low lighting he'd be able to watch Donna without being observed.

Immediately, things seemed to be going well. The women started out with polite chitchat. By the time they'd finished their first drink, the talk had moved on to neighborhood gossip. By the end of the second drink, they were giggling.

He loved to watch Donna laugh. It was even more special because he'd seen it so rarely.

"Now that we've talked of everyone else, tell me—what's the scuttlebutt on me?" Nola asked with a sly smile.

Donna shook her head. "No you don't! The last thing I'm going to do is insult the only person in Hilldale who actually has no hidden agenda with me."

Nola stirred her martini with her olive. "Oh? How do you know that?"

"Well, first of all, you haven't asked me to serve on any committees. Nor have you asked me to babysit." Donna leaned in closer. "And thankfully, you haven't asked me about my husband."

"And I won't, either." Nola held out her hand for Donna to shake.

What the hell, Jack wondered. Is Nola too drunk to remember the whole purpose of why we're here?

He was just about to give her the high sign when Donna said, "Frankly, there's not much to say. Hell, you live across the street. You've seen it for yourself. He's...gone."

Donna's mouth tightened.

As if that could hold back her tears.

If it's this easy to get her to spill the beans, she'll never be able to work for Acme, he thought.

He didn't know whether to be glad or disappointed.

"Well, hey, not to fret." Nola patted her hand. "It's just another way of bringing home the bacon, right?"

"Yes...right." Donna shrugged. "I admire you, Nola. You obviously want to live your life in a manner that suits you, and live it where it suits you—to hell with what others say."

"Darn tootin.'" Nola gave her a thumbs-up.

"Is that why you have a boarder now—because money is tight?"

Fuck it, Jack thought. She's seen me? How? Where?

Nola looked up. Involuntarily her eyes caught Jack's in the mirror. "A...boarder? What do you mean, dear?"

"Oh, you don't have to worry. I'm not going to tell anyone. It's nobody's business." Donna took a sip of her wine, but her eyes never went off Nola. "Like you say, we all have to pay the bills."

"Okay, yes...I do have someone staying with me—but just temporarily. A friend of a friend. He needed a place to stay."

"It doesn't matter! It's really none of my business." Donna leaned back. "Is he cute?"

"Who, Ja—I mean, Jason?" Nola shrugged. "He grows on you. I mean, it's just platonic. Like you said, roomies. You've seen him, right? Is that how you knew he was there?"

"Not really, no. I see his shadow, sometimes, when he stands by the window. It's as if he's always there, like a hermit." Donna looked down at her drink, which was almost empty. "Doesn't that bother you?"

"Dirty dishes in the sink bother me. A raised toilet seat bothers me. Doing someone else's laundry bothers the hell out of me—"

Jack frowned. How did this little girl's night turn into an I Hate Jack gripe session? Okay, yeah, maybe I left the toilet seat up once or twice, but that other stuff—

It was then he realized they weren't talking about Carl anymore.

Donna had turned the tables on Nola.

Jack laughed out loud.

He had half a mind to send them a drink with his compliments, but apparently he'd been beaten to the punch. Drinks had just been delivered. The waitress pointed over to a couple of guys—big strapping dudes in nice suits, sitting at the bar.

When the women looked up, the men waved.

Nola nodded slightly, but it wasn't an invitation.

The men didn't see it that way. They heaved themselves off their barstools and sauntered over.

Donna ignored them, but Nola looked and smiled. "Not now, boys. We're having a little girl talk."

The guys sat down anyway—one beside each of the women. The one closest to Nola—the slighter built of the two men, put his arm around her shoulder. "Quit being such a tease."

Her eyes narrowed. "I'm not. Take the hint."

"You're too beautiful to be angry."

"You're too stupid to take a hint," she growled at him. To make sure he got the message loud and clear, she poured her drink in his lap.

The man leaped up, cursing. "Fucking bitch!"

Nola and Donna jumped up, grabbing their purses. The other man grabbed Donna's arm. "Just because your girlfriend is frigid doesn't mean you have to be, too." He yanked her down onto him. "Come sit on papa's lap."

She looked him directly in the eyes and leaned in.

Before he knew it, she had him cupped in her right hand. She tightened up on him, twisting so hard that he gasped. "Gentlemen, the night is still young," Donna purred sweetly. "If you want to walk out of here upright—for that matter, if you want leave the same gender as when you came into this bar, then I would suggest that we part ways amicably." She gave him a hard twist as proof she meant business.

This time, when they rose to go, the men stayed put.

JACK WAITED UNTIL DONNA'S BEDROOM LIGHT WENT OUT BEFORE slipping back into Nola's house.

He wasn't surprised to find Nola waiting up for him. Before he could say a word, she said, "Jack, I know how you feel about Donna joining Acme, but I've got to say, she more than held her own tonight! If he pushed his luck, I truly believe she would have taken him out—"

"Nola really—you don't have to sell me. I was there. I saw it all."

"No, you didn't see her face, Jack! It was like...steel." She winced. "If I didn't know better, I'd think she was enjoying it."

He didn't say anything. What could he say?

Yes, he saw the look on her face.

It was the look of someone who had nothing to lose.

It was the look of a coldhearted killer.

He left a text for Ryan, telling him he'd be in the office by noon.

He packed his bag and went to bed.

For the first time in a while, he didn't dream of Donna.

When he woke, he knew the Donna of his dreams didn't really exist.

17

MICE vs. RASCLS

Back in the day, when the CIA recruited its agents, assets and operatives, it looked for certain emotional criteria that could be summed up in the acronym, MICE—that is money, ideology, coercion, and ego.

The terms are self-explanatory. That said, persons of interest who are motivated by any of these factors would be ripe for the plucking and training as spies.

(The "c" and the "e" may also stand for compromise *and* extortion. *As with most of the spy world, one must always leave room for flexibility, depending on the circumstances—even as it pertains to mnemonics.)*

Staying in step with the times, today's CIA has honed its wish list, now relying on these six influential factors, which go by the acronym RASCLS, and involve: reciprocation *(extending a kindness because human nature is driven to pay it back, if not forward);* authority *(belief comes with respect to those who invite you to play, and in proving one's self to them, and being rewarded with authority of your own);* scarcity *("This is your chance, it's now or never...");* commitment *(to the cause, proven during an ongoing series of more important actions);* liking *(welcome to our exclusive little club!), and* social proof *(proving one's commitment with public acts).*

In other words, they will always find a way to get you off the other side and onto theirs — those little RASCLS.

"The time has come," Ryan declared, in a voice that told Jack he didn't want any further discussion about it. "You and Emma have done a superior job in vetting Donna. She and I are scheduled to have our monthly catch-up lunch today. I'll ask her then."

Jack shrugged. At this juncture, he knew better than to argue about it. "Is she making you lunch?"

"If it's her infamous chicken pot pie, I think it's time you tell her you're bringing a few guests along," Emma piped up.

Ryan turned to her. "How would you know how tasty it is?"

Emma's mouth fell open. "Um…I think I read about it, in one of our reconnaissance reports." Emma rummaged through a file. "In fact, I'm sure you mentioned it—"

She's covering for Arnie, Jack thought. Interesting. Talk about an odd couple.

"I've never mentioned it." Ryan's eyes shifted from Emma to Jack.

Jack laughed. "It was in a report—with Arnie. What can I say? During the black bag mission. The poor guy was starving, and there were leftovers. Don't worry, Ryan, I made sure he only took a spoonful."

"Oh yeah? I've eaten with him. It's as if every meal is his last." Ryan muttered. "This is one mission I'm glad is finally over."

You and me both, Jack thought. He smiled at Ryan. "Good luck. I stand firm with my assertion—she'll say no."

"If she does, she's not the woman I thought she was."

"So, she's another kind of woman—one who's sane, and has her priorities straight."

"You've spent all this time learning what you can about her, and you're still blind to the one thing that drives her, eh?" Ryan shook his head, awed. "That Benjamin is as good as mine. It'll be like taking candy from a baby. If you're going to tag along, we've got to hurry so that you can position yourself somewhere she can't be struck dumb by your boyish good looks."

Hearing that, Emma snorted.

Jack had half a mind to tell Ryan the truth about the chicken pot pie. As a dog person, Ryan wouldn't appreciate the fact that Lassie took the fall.

FROM WHAT JACK COULD SEE AND HEAR FROM THE NEXT BOOTH, Ryan did a good job dodging her very specific questions about the investigation, focusing instead on more mundane topics, like Mary's grades, Jeff's last ball game, and Trisha's latest growth milestone. Jack knew his boss had to do this because the investigation was ongoing, and Donna didn't have the clearance status required to get the straight scoop.

Not yet, anyway.

He hoped that time would come only after the Quorum had been wiped off the face of the Earth.

Tatyana's demise was a step in the right direction.

From the troubled look on her face, Jack knew she'd heard Ryan's patter before—and was tired of it. She wanted him to get to the point of the meeting:

What progress was Acme making in finding the Quorum?

Still, Donna kept her impatience to herself and played along. "The children are okay," she assured Ryan. "They don't ask about Carl as much as they did, you know, since Phyllis—"

"Look, I'm sorry she told them that way. I know how hard it's been for you."

"Oh, no, you don't." Her words were cool, her smile frigid.

She was calling his bluff.

"You know we're doing everything we can. Seriously, Donna, I wish I could do more—" As Ryan paused, his eyes shifted away.

She tensed up.

Wow, thought Jack, considering Ryan's poker face, she's certainly pretty good at reading body language.

"—Particularly since I've been ordered to stop Carl's paychecks after next month." Ryan shifted uneasily in the café's hard plastic chair. "You see, because of all the recent terror threats, other things have taken priority—"

Donna sat still for a moment as that sunk in.

But she didn't break out in tears, or even shout angrily at him.

Instead she let loose with a humorless laugh. "Well, well, isn't that the cherry on the cake of my day! So tell me, Ryan: just what am I supposed to do now? Sell the house, get some secretarial job, and put my kids in after-school daycare?" Her questions were laced in acid.

Jack remembered the estimate she received for Mary's braces, as well as the bill she got from Jeff's podiatrist for his orthotics. And with Carl never having been declared dead, a widow's pension wasn't in her future, either.

"Frankly, I for one think that would be an incredible waste of your natural talents." Ryan paused then added, "Why not come and work for me?"

"You're being funny, right?" If so, Donna wasn't laughing.

Jack hoped that meant she wasn't considering it, either.

Ryan shook his head. "I'm being perfectly serious, Donna. I've got a gut feeling that you'd make a pretty good field op. First of all, you're in great shape, and you're a crack shot–"

She frowned. "Yeah, but come on, Ryan. We both know that there's more to Acme than that."

"Of course there is." By the way he leaned forward, Jack could tell that he was just warming to the subject. "I'm not claiming that it will be a cakewalk by any means. Like all our operatives, you'll have to go through some pretty rigorous training. And yeah, sure, sometimes the work can be dangerous. But it's also challenging. Meaningful. And certainly more fulfilling than...well, you know."

"Yeah, I know. More 'fulfilling' than being a housewife, right?" she declared sarcastically. One sharp glance from him had her pursing her lips in order to keep from saying anything else. "Look, um, Ryan, I can't say that I'm not flattered that you'd even consider me. But–well, I guess I don't see what it is that you see in me."

"Frankly, Donna, your best feature is that you'd be highly motivated—"

Donna knew what he meant, and so did Jack:

Highly motivated to kill. To avenge Carl.

She'd also be highly motivated to stay alive, he thought, if not for her own sake, then for Mary, Jeff, and little Trisha.

"—and of course, there will be the satisfaction of knowing that you'll be helping us take down the bastards who took out Carl."

Jack shook his head. Translation: You'll get the closure you so desperately need.

As if. Don't believe him, Donna. The wound may close, but the memory of its pain stays with you for a lifetime.

But wasn't watching her children as they slept in their beds—all snuggled in, safe and sound–satisfaction enough? Wasn't it enough that they'd already lost one parent?

Donna must have been thinking the same thing as she murmured, "Ryan, I ...I can't. I guess I'm not as strong as you think."

That brought the faintest smile to Ryan's lips. "Oh, I don't know about that." He tossed down a couple of twenties on the table and stood up to leave. "Look, there's no rush. Don't give me an answer today. All I'm asking is that you think about it, okay?"

She shrugged and stared down at the money on the table.

When she lifted her head, it was in Jack's direction. There was a faraway look in her eye.

And just the slightest smile on her lips.

His heart lurched when it dawned on him: *she's seriously considering his offer.*

Maybe he was wrong about her. Maybe she wouldn't think anything at all about trading elementary school volunteering and endless baskets of dirty laundry and all the work that went with cooking three meals for her children—not to mention cleaning the house yet one more time—for the bone-chilling thrills that working at a place like Acme would offer her.

Maybe she'd give up her quiet, safe life in a second, to assure herself that Carl didn't die in vain.

He prayed that wasn't the case.

The answer to his prayer came a moment later, when the light went out of her eyes. She shook her head firmly, as if confirming her final decision on the issue.

Good, because Donna didn't need to avenge Carl's death. She had Jack to do it for her.

Of course, she didn't know this—not yet, anyway.

She wouldn't either, until he accomplished that very goal.

Jack waited until Donna drove off before joining Ryan in his car.

Ryan had the cash in his hand and handed it to Jack. He shrugged. "I guess you were right, after all."

He slid out of Ryan's car and walked over to his rental.

Jack knew he should be happy with the outcome, but for some reason, he wasn't. Maybe it was the feeling he had when he saw Donna waver over her decision.

Still, she'd made the right one. He had no doubt about it.

If only she felt the same way.

Before he left town, Jack drove by Donna's house.

He found her standing in the backyard, beside the clothesline. She had a laundry basket at her side. He watched as she bent to pick up something and clip it onto the line. Like most of the items already hooked and flapping in the gentle breeze, it was a bright white cloth diaper.

When she was done, she eased herself into one of the two white Adirondack chairs under the large shady oak tree.

He knew the second one had been Carl's.

He wished he could sit there beside her.

He watched as she took a newspaper from the basket. From what he could see, the section she was reading wasn't news, or lifestyle. It was the classifieds.

She's looking for a job, he realized. In this lousy economy, what is she qualified for? She married right out of college, and started popping out babies. She never worked in an office. She's the first to admit her typing skills are lousy. I guess she can be a waitress.

Jolene Caruthers came to mind. He winced at the thought of Donna hustling for tips to make ends meet—to pay the mortgage, and for healthcare, and for the added expense of after-school daycare for her kids while she finished her shifts.

Granted, other single mothers had similar financial burdens. But because of him, this particular mother was now in dire straits.

Suddenly, he felt ashamed about the fake inheritance ploy he'd used with her aunt, Phyllis.

He knew how to fix it. By next week, Phyllis's niece

would soon tell her the good news that she was the recipient of a monthly stipend, the legacy of a trust from the long lost friend on her father's side. And that—surprise, surprise—it covered the monthly mortgage note, and there was enough left over to meet the family's other expenses as well.

The moment he got back to Paris, he'd make sure to set up a blind trust, and an automatic transfer from his own savings.

As he drove off, he looked at her one last time in his side view mirror and watched as she removed her sunglasses so that she could wipe away a tear.

She hadn't made the wrong decision. But the only way she'd realize that is if the people who had killed her husband were behind bars, or dead as well.

From now on, this would be his mission:

He'd be the one to avenge Carl for her. He'd take down the Quorum so that she could move on.

When she could do so, he'd be waiting for her.

18

The Take

Information collected during an intelligence operation is called "the take." Sometimes it ends up in an asset or agent's dossier. Sometimes it ends up in a dead file.

But are files ever truly dead? Even when a mission has ended or an agent or asset dies, do the memories and experiences and encounters collated in her dossier cease to exist as well?

IT ANNOYED JACK TO NO END TO FIND A LADY FRIEND'S THONG tangled up in his sheets. No matter how small and lacy, they were inevitably some color—red, hot pink, deep purple, electric blue—that would turn the rest of his laundry the same silly hue.

Whenever this happened, he didn't know who was more embarrassed, he or Marie, the new laundress he'd hired now that he was back in Paris. She pinked up whenever she handed over the guilty garment.

He had half a mind to tell her to keep them, but he knew better than to ask a former nun if ass floss was her kind of thing.

He could have tossed them out. In fact, maybe he should have done so, since he never called the same woman back, but he hated the thought of someone rummaging through his garbage bin and finding them.

Instead, they went in a drawer.

Since leaving Los Angeles, he'd slept with a different woman each night. He winced when he thought of what Acme's psych investigator would think of this. He could imagine the man writing, *Trophies?*

Okay, yeah, maybe.

He'd been cuckolded. Screwing other women in the bed he once shared with his ex wasn't exactly payback, but it was damn close.

Also in the drawer was her lover's boxer briefs.

The joker had walked out of there commando.

The asshole knew exactly what he was doing.

He wasn't just fucking her, Jack thought. He was fucking with me, too.

Someday, he'd learn the name of the clown.

As far as the panty drawer was concerned, it was time to clean house. Not only would the thongs go to *Armée du Salut* —Paris' version of the Salvation Army—so would anything else that didn't matter anymore.

He looked around for an empty box. There was one under his desk—

Only it wasn't empty. It held one thing: Donna Stone's recipe book.

Somehow he'd forgotten to return it with the rest of the

evidence he'd taken during his background investigation of her. He'd barely scanned through it. After all, didn't most women write their personal thoughts in a diary instead?

He opened it. Flipping through the pages, he noticed that all the recipes were in her handwriting. He'd know it anywhere.

Toward the back was one in which the tab was labeled *Carl's Favorite Beef Stew*. He turned to it.

The tipoff that Donna had not used it since Carl's death was the envelope stuck in the fold. It wasn't in Donna's handwriting, but in Carl's.

The flap wasn't sealed, but tucked inside the envelope. He opened it:

Dear Donna,

If you're reading this, it's because I couldn't come home to you, as I planned.

Please don't think it's because I didn't want to, or that I didn't try my damnedest to do so. My intention was, and has always been to be the best husband in the world, and the best father to our sweet, wonderful children. My leaving was the only way in which I could guarantee your safety, and theirs.

I have no doubt that somewhere—hopefully on this earth, and soon—we'll be reunited. When we are, I'll make good on the promise I made on our wedding day: to spend the rest of eternity with the woman I love.

Yours, always,

Carl

Jack stared down at the note for a long time. Finally, he

put it back in the envelope, which he slipped back between the pages of the recipe book.

He knew he had to get this back to Donna.

He'd only been gone from Acme headquarters for less than a week, but Ryan had him booked on the next morning's flight out of Charles De Gaulle for a debriefing on an important extermination. He'd take the book along and hand it off to Ryan.

As he flipped through the recipes, Donna's voice played out in his mind.

He remembered her deep chuckle, her sly smile, even the sadness in her eyes.

Damn it, he missed her. Not that she'd ever know this.

Because she'd never know about him. By passing on the transfer, he'd made sure of that.

Even if somehow their paths were to cross, he knew she'd never love anyone but Carl.

Especially after she read this letter.

At least it got his mind out of the thong drawer, if only for a moment.

Jack stared down at the drawer then slammed it shut. He'd walk down to the shelter another day. He had to pack for Los Angeles.

"Sure, now that the investigation is over, feel free to walk it over to Donna," Ryan said to him, without batting an eye.

Was he joking? "She doesn't know of my existence," Jack

sputtered. "How would I explain why a complete stranger has her recipe book?"

Ryan shrugged. "No one told you to take it in the first place. If you feel it should be returned, it's your problem, not Acme's."

"So, I'm supposed to knock on her front door, and hand it over by saying, 'I'm the guy who vetted you for the Acme gig you turned down?'"

Ryan winced. "It's certainly not the route I'd take. She didn't even know she was being investigated. It might make her feel a wee bit…threatened. "

Jack knew Ryan was referring to the incident with the serial killer, McInnis.

They both knew what happened when Donna got angry. Not a pretty sight.

"If you feel it's important to do, you'll figure something out." Ryan waved away Jack's consternation. "But do it on your own time—which is not any time in the next forty-eight hours." He tossed a folder in front of Jack. "A Mexican drug lord, Arturo Rodriguez, is getting married this weekend. According to the border guard he's paid off, he's having his bachelor party on this side of the fence—the Aero Club, in San Diego. He's booked it for tomorrow night under the name of 'Mr. Jones and party.' The Mexican government wants it to look like a heart attack. The DEA hopes we can oblige, so that we cut off any notions of retaliation."

Jack nodded, taking it all in.

Sort of. What he was really thinking about was how he might be able to sneak the recipe book back into some unopened box in her garage.

He'd climb over the far backyard wall, enter the garage through the side door, and be out in no time. Piece of cake.

Then he'd head down to San Diego to take care of Rodriguez, which would be a bit harder, what with all his bodyguards, and it being a public place—not to mention it would have to look like natural causes.

Mrs. Stone had made the right decision to stay out of the game.

Maybe it was time for him to cash in his chips as well.

HE WAS NOT ALONE.

He'd just gotten up on the brick wall when he saw the figure emerge from the little girl's playhouse in the middle of the yard.

What...the hell?

Jack went flat on the wall. It was a full moon, but whoever it was hadn't seen him—not yet, anyway. The man, dressed in black, had a ski mask over his face, and was wearing infrared goggles.

He was also holding a semiautomatic rifle.

As the man made his way to the back door that led into the kitchen, Jack slipped over the wall—

Landing in a pile of leaves.

The intruder had just opened the screen door when he heard the crunch of leaves and turned around.

Jack dropped onto his belly. Despite having a suppressor on his Glock 21, the last thing he wanted to do was have a shoot-out in Donna's backyard.

The other guy wasn't so concerned. The man's head

turned as he scanned the yard. Jack didn't move a muscle. Hell, he didn't breathe. But when the man raised his rifle and aimed directly at him, Jack knew he'd been spotted.

He was a sitting duck.

Jack saw the flash from a gun—not from the rifle, but from another gun pointed out the French door of the upstairs balcony, off the master bedroom.

Donna shot at the intruder.

She must have hit him, too, because the man groaned in pain. It wasn't a fatal shot because he stumbled toward the wooden picnic table, upturning it and ducking behind it just as a second shot ricocheted off one of its planks.

It took the intruder a second to realize what was happening. When he did, he shot back at her. She must have ducked, but he was spooked enough that it gave Jack the few crucial seconds he needed to pull out his gun.

That's when he heard the child crying inside the house. It must have been the youngest daughter, Trisha. Had she been hit with a ricocheting bullet?

A second later, the yard and house lit up, and an alarm wailed.

The guy limped away, through the side of the yard.

Jack didn't follow. Donna's security system was hooked up to the Hilldale police. A symphony of police sirens could already be heard. They were getting closer by the second. A single man trying to leave the gated community, either by car or on foot, would surely be questioned.

From his cell, he called Nola's phone. She picked up after three rings.

"House of Utopia," she answered in a singsong voice.

"I'm parked in the White BMW sedan in the alley

between Avery and Maple. Meet me there so that you can escort me out of the ruckus."

Nola let loose with a husky chuckle. "I thought you'd never ask."

By the time she strolled into the alley, the sirens had stopped, but even from where he stood he could hear the hum of the crowd milling around the police cars in front of Donna's house.

Nola hopped in beside him. "Did you set off Donna's alarm?"

"Yes, but I wasn't alone. Someone almost did a B and E on the Widow Stone's place—and he was packing heat."

"You think it's the Quorum, don't you?"

Jack nodded.

Nola pursed her lips. "I'm sorry I didn't catch it on the monitor. But a girl's got to take a shower sometime—"

"Don't blame yourself. The place has been a graveyard for a year now. I wish Donna's dog, Lassie, was a real watch-dog. Arnie and I had no problems making friends. She didn't even bark at the shooter in the backyard."

Nola shivered. "And they say it's safer in Suburbia. Ha! These houses sit on almost full-acre lots. Even if you're able to scream, no one will hear you. I'm going to requisition an attack dog from Acme. One with sharp fangs. A German shepherd."

"I'm sure Ryan won't have a problem with that." He started the car's engine. "I guess we can't avoid the hubbub, since it's the only way to the security gate. Once we're a few blocks beyond it, I'll let you out, and you can walk home."

Her mouth puckered into a pout. "And you call this a real date?"

Nola sat close enough to put her arm around his shoulder. When they drove slowly past the crowd, she muttered, "Slow down and look the other way while I speak to an old boyfriend."

The beau was one of the cops on crowd control. He lit up when he saw her.

"What's all the fuss, handsome?" she asked sweetly.

He frowned to see her with a male companion, but when she smiled up at him, he only had eyes for her. "Your neighbor across the street had a possum or something set off her alarm. At least, that's what she thinks."

So, Donna was doing her bit and covering for Acme, Jack realized.

"See what passes for excitement in these parts?" Nola pouted out loud before upping the wattage on her smile tenfold. "Speaking of excitement, don't be such a stranger, Officer. You know how I feel about hard...metal."

Jack sighed as he rolled down the street. "You never fail to amaze me," he muttered.

She nodded, satisfied. "That's what they all say."

HE'D JUST HIT THE 405 GOING SOUTH WHEN HE REMEMBERED HE still had the box he'd taken from Donna's Aunt Phyllis. If Donna ever went looking for her recipe book, even if she couldn't find it in her own garage maybe she'd remember her aunt's pack rat mentality and check the old lady's garage. Besides, Phyllis' house was in Pasadena, right off the I-10. From there, he could hit the road to the I-5 and take it south into San Diego for the fun and games of the Rodriguez hit.

I can't believe Ryan would think Donna would find this sort of life exciting, he thought. But he had to admit, it beat hanging diapers out to dry.

19

Bona Fides

The items carried on an agent as proof of his claimed identity is called his "bone fides."

It may be formal identification, such as a driver's license, a passport, a marriage license, or an employee pass—all forged.

It may be photos of an agent, digitally altered to superimpose images of him with others of merit, who, in reality, he's never met before.

It may be written endorsements from others.

So, how do you know if the person you meet is "the real thing?"

Assume the worst. Ask questions later.

That way, your heart stays in one piece.

Welcome to Relationship 101.

BY THE TIME HE CIRCUMNAVIGATED LA'S HIGHWAYS TO PHYLLIS' tiny cottage in Pasadena, it was after two o'clock. As he'd hoped, the house was dark and still inside. The door to the garage wasn't even locked.

He found one of the boxes marked SHIVES, nudged aside the tape holding it shut, and crammed the recipe book deep inside. Just as he slid it back onto the shelf, he was hit with the glaring garage light.

Aunt Phyllis stood there with a baseball bat in her hand. "Jeez, guy! You're lucky you're not a raccoon." She squinted at him. "Who the hell are you, and what are you doing in here?"

"We met when I was doing the research on your...er... sister's husband. For my client's last will and testament." Jack gave her a wide smile and prayed she'd remember.

Aunt Phyllis squinted even harder. "Ah! You're that guy? Heck, wouldn't have known you if I passed you on the street. I'm blind as a bat without my glasses."

"You'd given me some mementos and I wanted to make sure to return them to you." He pointed at the box now holding Donna's cookbook.

She frowned. "At two in the morning?"

"I'm leaving town. You were my last stop." He knew better than to lie to her, even without the bat in her hand. "You're right, I guess I could have left it on the front stoop, or in the mailbox or something, but I was worried that it was too important to just leave anywhere." He reached out with it.

She took it with one hand. The other took his hand and squeezed it. "I want to thank you for finding my niece. I guess you know she was the heir apparent after all! In fact, she got the first check just yesterday. It couldn't have come at a better time for the poor thing. You see, her husband left her

—just took off out of the blue—and she's been paralyzed with grief." She shook her head angrily. "Maybe having a little financial independence will give her the gumption to admit it to herself and get on with her life."

Jack patted her on the back. "Well, then, I'm glad to hear that they moved on the paperwork as quickly as they did. I guess I should let you get some shut-eye. Good night, Ms. Lindholm."

She held onto his hand and murmured coquettishly, "You know, my original offer still stands."

"You mean…" Aw heck, he thought, is she coming onto me? If I insult her, I've got to duck fast. She's still holding that bat—

"Yes, silly! Of course I do!" Seeing his shocked face, she added, "You know—introduce you formally, to my niece."

As much as he'd love that more than anything in the world, he knew he couldn't.

There would come a time.

Hopefully, sooner rather than later.

"I get it," she said with a giggle. "You like playing hard to get. That's okay," She looked at her watch. "Before you take off, you can at least come in for a piece of pie. In fact"— she grinned slyly—"Donna made it herself."

He thought about it for a moment. What the heck? He'd never see this woman again.

For that matter, he'd probably never see Donna again, either.

He had nothing to lose. And yes, he was hungry. If spending an hour with her aunt was as close as he was going to get to her at this point in their lives, then so be it.

"Do you know what goes great with pie?" Phyllis asked.

When he shook his head, she sighed rhapsodically. "Martinis! I'll whip up a batch of those as well...Young man, it's not polite to laugh at a woman my age. In an hour you'll soon find out I'm a lot funnier after I have a drink or two in me. Hey, if you play your cards right, you might get another story or two out of me, about Donna—not that I'm trying to set you two up or anything..."

~

JACK'S HEAD FELT AS IF HE'D BEEN KO'ED WITH A sledgehammer. He opened one eye, and found himself staring at the ceiling.

It wasn't the ceiling of his Venice Beach apartment, either.

Moving his neck was just too damn painful so he focused on the pattern of the ceiling tiles until he realized he had somehow made it back to Acme headquarters.

He breathed a sigh of relief that he wasn't in Phyllis Lindholm's house either. He didn't know how he'd let her talk him into all those dirty martinis. During Donna's vetting, had he known how many war stories Phyllis had about her niece, he would have just come over with a bottle of Grey Goose, some vermouth, and a jar of pimento-stuffed olives, then hit the record app on his iPhone and let her chatter on. It would have saved Emma at least a week of research.

Even now, one story in particular—about some boy who'd gotten fresh with Donna while she was a freshman in high school, and how she'd dealt with him—seemed so fresh in his memory, so real to him, that he could actually hear Donna's voice in his head.

But then he realized he wasn't imagining it.

She was there, in the room with him.

He lifted his head to discover he was sprawled out on one of Acme's conference room tables. He was alone, and the door was shut. So, why was he hearing Donna's voice?

Then he saw her—with Ryan, through a two-way mirror. They were sitting across the table from each other in the conference room on the other side of the wall.

What the hell was she doing there?

"I want in." This time, there was no hesitation in her voice.

"Hmmm. Well..." Ryan's words trailed off, and he blinked. Twice. Then he frowned.

Jack breathed a sigh of relief. Good, he sees it as a sign that she's fickle, and he's not going to give in.

Donna must have realized this too. Arching a brow, she muttered, "Don't tell me you're having second thoughts about the offer! What, have you filled your mommy quota for the month or something?"

"Part of your charm has always been your sense of humor. No, Donna, we are always on the lookout for good field ops. And quite frankly, I can't think of a better candidate for what we need. Your 'mommy' status is the perfect cover. And the fact that you already know how to shoot is a bonus, but–" He stopped abruptly. "Tell me, Donna, have you ever killed anyone?"

Her eyes flashed angrily, but she kept her cool and forced a shrug. "No. Why do you ask?"

"Because once you make the decision to join Acme,

there's no looking back," Ryan warned her. "I just want you to be perfectly sure that you won't regret the choice you're about to make."

She didn't speak. She didn't have to. The little telltale signs Jack knew so well were all there. When the pupils of her eyes darkened a shade, she had dredged up a past hurt. The tip of her tongue through her lips was her shorthand for determination. Whenever she pushed the hair behind her right ear, she signaled she was ready to move on, with no regrets.

As these three signs played out before him, he realized that no matter how badly he wanted to protect her, he couldn't stop her from what she had to do:

Take down Carl's killers.

To do that, she'd need Acme.

And yes, Acme needed her, too. The way she handled herself with the killer in the yard was proof enough of that.

Affiliating with Acme will keep her from being the last thing she wants to be—a victim, Jack thought.

He could understand that perfectly.

He realized, right then and there, that he had no right to stand in her way; that no matter how badly he wanted to protect her from others, he couldn't protect her from herself.

"My bottom line is this, Ryan—I'm not spending the rest of my life as a victim. All I'm asking is that you give me a chance. It's the least you can do." Donna said it in the same tone she used on her children when she wanted to make it clear to them, in no uncertain terms, that they weren't going to get their way.

Then she rose and started for the door.

Donna had almost reached the threshold when she felt

Ryan's hand on her arm. "Okay, tell you what. Come back tomorrow, say, around ten. I'll put you on the shooting range to see if you're as good as Carl claimed. Then we'll take it from there."

She was wearing that take-no-prisoners smile Jack had come to know and love. "That will work. Trisha is at her nursery school until two."

She shook his hand. Then, impulsively, she gave him a kiss on the cheek too.

Ryan blushed bright red.

Jack laughed out loud.

She certainly knows how to play him, Jack thought. I would have made her work a little harder for it.

Almost as if he'd heard Jack, Ryan tapped his side of the mirror then motioned for Jack to join him.

So, he knows I'm in here, Jack thought. That's just…great.

He rolled off the conference room table and onto his feet. Time to face the music.

He walked in to find Ryan staring out the window. Without turning around to look at Jack, he said, "Grab a seat. Sorry we woke you."

"It was worth it." Jack puckered up and made a kissing sound.

Ryan shrugged. "You're jealous."

"You're right. And you're going to regret the decision to hire her." He reached in his pocket for his wallet and took out the one-hundred dollar bill Ryan had handed him just the other day.

Ryan held it up. "Want to go double or nothing on that?"

Jack smiled. "You're on." Jack pocketed the bill. "I'll need it to cover expenses tonight, in San Diego."

Ryan snorted. "From what I've heard about the girls in that club, you'll need more than that. See my assistant about petty cash."

As Jack hit the threshold, Ryan added, "Jack, remember —if Donna makes it all the way, it's because she wants it that badly."

Jack nodded, but he didn't look back.

BY THE TIME JACK MADE IT BACK UP TO LOS ANGELES, RYAN had Donna's shooting range targets hanging in his office. Beside all the perfect bulls eyes to the heart, there were a couple where the groin area had been blown to smithereens.

That gave Jack a reason to smile.

Ryan didn't say a word as he watched Jack's eyes take this in, but the smirk on his face said it all: upping the ante had paid off.

Ryan was just as proud about her perfect physical, clean-as-a-whistle background check, and her passing the psych evaluation.

Jack shook his head in disgust. Out of the corner of his mouth, he muttered to Emma, "Looks like teacher's got a new pet."

"Frankly, I'll be ecstatic if she's able to go all the way at the Farm," Emma declared. "What happened to Carl was sad. And the way she found out was awful! I can understand her wanting to be in on whatever it is we have to do to take the Quorum down." Emma stopped, as if she'd just thought of something. "Hey, if she does, I'll finally get to meet her, face-to-face. And you will, too."

He shrugged. If Donna ever knew the role he played in Carl's murder, he'd be the last person she'd ever want to meet.

The only way to make it up to her was to take down the Quorum.

He had a lot of work in front of him.

20

Sere

SERE stands for survival, evasion, resistance, and escape. It is the acronym for a US military program in which military personnel, private military contractors and Department of Defense employees are trained in survival skills as well as evading capture. Most of those who take this course are either military aircrew or special ops personnel who are deemed a high risk for capture.

SERE is not a weekend at Bernie's. Nor is it a gal pal getaway. There are no bromances involved, and certainly no sex on the beach.

Although, if you're in the middle of the woods and it's pouring rain and the temperature drops below forty degrees, you won't object to snuggling in the fetal position with two of your teammates. In fact, for once in your life you may insist on being the ham in a sandwich threesome.

JACK HADN'T PLANNED ON STOPPING BY THE US NAVY'S Training Site in Warner Springs, California but as it happened, he discovered that one of its officers, Dan Forthye, recently had a run-in with Pinky Ring.

He was told to report first to the base commander, Captain Raymond Nichols, who was watching an extreme interrogation exercise. He'd never met Captain Nichols, but knew his reputation as an exceptional covert-ops instructor, especially in SERE skills.

Jack was led to a cinder block building on the outskirts of the base.

The room in which they were standing was small, and had a two-way mirror that looked into a larger room where a mock water boarding interrogation was in session.

The flashing strobe lights in the darkened room made it difficult to see what exactly was going on. Despite this, and the fact that the tortured candidate's head was covered with a black burlap bag and arms and legs were trussed firmly to a board slanted downward, he could tell the person was a woman. Sure, she was broad-shouldered, lean and like everyone else attending Warner Springs, she more than likely had shed all excess body fat within the first four weeks. In truth, the giveaway was more obvious: she had a great set of knockers.

Unfortunately for her, this didn't throw her torturers off their game.

In fact, it seemed to make them even more determined to break her.

She refused to make it easy for them. Granted, her body tensed up, if only slightly and for a mere second, whenever the head of the board was tilted downward in anticipation of the water that would soon drench the cloth over her face.

When it came down on her, it was fierce and steady, along with the taunts and threats from her torturers.

No matter how loud the audio loop of crying babies rico-cheted through the room, or how hair-raising her captors' shouts and jibes, the captive went Zen on them.

No screaming, let alone whimpering or crying.

It was almost as if she were asleep.

Eventually, she succumbed to the need to take in air. Considering the low angle of her head, it was inevitable that she'd suck in so much water through her nose and her mouth that she'd be forced to cough in an attempt to stop the drowning sensation.

Instead, she drew the water up into her lungs—

Until she blacked out.

"Damn it!" growled one of her torturers. "That's the fourth time the bitch has passed out on us." Frustrated as to what should be their next move, he glanced over at the mirror.

Raymond tapped it with his knuckles.

The interrogators exchanged glum glances before releasing the woman's bindings and pulling the sack off her head.

It took a moment for Jack to realize the woman was Donna Stone.

"Shit," he murmured.

Whereas most of Donna's training was taking place at the Farm, other facilities around the country were better equipped to conduct Level C SERE courses, which simulated high-risk capture behind enemy lines.

Considering its proximity to LA, I should have figured Ryan would make sure she was sent here, he thought.

Raymond shook his head in awe. "You can say that again. This one is a real kamikaze. This is the last of seventeen counter-resistance tests, and so far she's aced every one. Her spy craft skills are incredible, too—and innate, from what I can tell. As for languages, her Spanish and French are more than passable. Her German needs a little work. Had a tough time with Arabic, but who doesn't? And boy, can she shoot."

Having seen her in action, Jack could only nod in agreement.

Her interrogators slapped her until she regained consciousness, at which point she rolled off the board and onto all fours in order to choke out the rest of the water in her lungs.

When her heaving stopped, one of her interrogators offered his hand to get her on her feet.

She smiled up at him, but rose on her own. When she was fully erect, she turned to the mirror.

She winked.

Jack's heart leaped in his chest. For a moment, he thought she'd seen him.

Even if she had, she wouldn't know him, he reasoned.

Raymond was flipping through the file folder in his hand. It had Donna's name on it. "Hey, I see here that she's one of your agents—and that you cleared her for Level C." He raised a brow. "So, are you two close?"

Jack knew what he was really asking. Ha, if only. He tried to keep from frowning. "In fact, we've never met."

Raymond looked down at the file, as if scrutinizing some

of Jack's chicken scratch for enlightenment on Donna. The slight smirk on his lips was a dead giveaway as to what he was really thinking: *What's wrong with this guy?*

Jack shrugged. "My job wasn't to get up close and personal. In fact, it was the exact opposite. But yes, she passed on our end, with flying colors."

Raymond nodded. "Well, you certainly read her right. She'd survive Armageddon."

"By that, I presume she did well during the survival course."

"I'll say! You'll get a kick out of what her instructors have to say when the file comes back your way." Raymond lifted the file in his hand. "She was the first to snare a squirrel. Then she fricasseed it! By all accounts, it was a hell of a feast, what with the herbs and edible plants she foraged up. And she was the only one on her team who wasn't grossed out at the thought of using a tampon as a survival tool. She took the cotton fiber for fire tinder and for water filtration, and used the wick for a pinesap candle. She even remembered to use the wrapper to keep their matches dry." He smiled. "Not only that, but she was the last one to emerge from her three days in solitary survival. Trust me, she was the only one who looked as if she'd come back from a spa weekend." Raymond chuckled. "Okay, maybe not exactly relaxed and refreshed. The years she spent as a Scouts' den mother really paid off."

"And yet she played rough when it was her turn to interrogate?"

Raymond's smile faded. "That's putting it mildly. Let me put it this way—after the results of her stint as a mock captor, I'd hate to be on her hit list."

"Why is that?"

"Usually, it's a three-day assignment. We took her off interrogation after the very first day—when she broke four candidates."

Jack frowned. "Was she being retaliatory?"

"No. I mean sure, she got the usual catcalls. But if you're asking if she was Tailhooked, no." Raymond shook his head. "Jack, you know how competitive these candidates can be. It's every man for himself—or woman. Not exactly kindergarten. Kumbaya is done back home, in their respective units."

In regard to Donna, that was a problem. By definition, assassins didn't work in cliques. Sure, certain missions were collaborations in which various agents worked their specialties. Apparently, Raymond recognized the fact that she was a woman of many talents.

That's exactly the point, Jack thought. She's not supposed to be anywhere but in cozy lazy little Hilldale.

Jack's eyes dropped to the manila folder. "I presume this includes a psych evaluation, too."

"Yes. When the evaluator asked her the typical questions as to how she's able to keep her cool, you know what she told him? That everything she sees here is something she's dealt with before—not on any battlefield, but as a mom. To her, covert ops are all fun and games—no different, really, than those you play with children. 'Isn't that what men are anyway, scared little boys, playing at war?' No one can get to her but her kids. And saving her kids is what drives her. The shrink wrote that she sees her time here as a real-life version of 'Survivor.' She wants to be the last man standing." Raymond frowned. "He suggested we take her off the assignment if we wanted to have a graduating class bigger than one—*her.*"

Which brought Jack to a question he was loath to ask. "Did she use any form of...coercion?"

They both knew he meant sex.

Raymond winced. "No, she didn't have to. With two of the guys, she stuck to the drill. With the third guy, she went all mommy dearest on his ass. She talked him onto the ledge by hitting on his irrational fears, then she sprinkled his mask as if she was blessing him with holy water. The dude felt those few drops and squealed like a piggy." Raymond rolled his eyes. "A State Department wonk. Frankly, I think the dude was a little disappointed that she didn't beat it out of him. I guess he thought this was some sort of fantasy spy camp or something."

"So, one of the broken candidates was a woman? How did that go?"

"Stone never even dampened the woman's mask. She just let the wailing baby soundtrack do the dirty work. Then she talked about what people really want in life, and how those who join covert-ops look to fill a hole inside themselves. She claimed she knew firsthand, and told the candidate not to follow in her footsteps. She asked the captive why she felt the need to be torn down by someone who didn't give a damn about her, only to be made into the image of someone who'd be used and abused by her own government. Then she described the process of drowning, and why it's a quicker way out of someone's perceived problems. Stone gave her a chance to 'reassess the situation.' That's how she put it. The captive reassessed, all right. Right after she left the Farm, she resigned from the State Department. In her exit interview, she claimed she was finally going to accept her boyfriend's proposal of marriage, make babies, and write romantic suspense novels."

Jack wondered, should Donna get the opportunity to avenge her husband's death, could she ever go back to the life of a suburban mom? For her sake, he hoped so, but he doubted it.

"We thought getting a taste of her own medicine would do the trick," Raymond continued. "We have ways of anticipating a benign response, and getting around it. As you see here, she knew what to expect and flipped it."

Jack thought, Why am I not surprised?

He left a benign smile on his head as he held out his hand to take his leave. "Thanks for your time and insights, Captain. Now, if you can tell me where I might find Captain Forsythe, I'll be on my way."

Raymond nodded out the door. "Father Forsythe is our chaplain now. A service is in session, but it should be ending soon. You'll find the chapel two blocks east, four doors down, on the right." He smirked. "Are you sure you don't you want to stick around to see how she handles the escape trials? That should be a 'come to Jesus' moment' for someone, if not her."

Jack shook his head. The thought of watching any more of Donna's transition into an assassin was something he couldn't stomach.

He blamed himself for it.

Besides, he knew her progress was being recorded in the dossier that would follow her back to Acme. Someday, he would access it. No time soon, though. Seeing what she'd become hurt too much.

He felt guilty for having played such a big role in her life. It certainly wasn't the role he would have chosen if they could have met under other circumstances.

The way it looked now, they'd never meet at all.

A SERVICE WAS GOING ON IN THE CHAPEL.

Jack waited the forty minutes, until it was over. It took another fifteen minutes for everyone to clear out. When he was certain it was empty, he entered.

To the left of the altar and just beyond a confessional booth was a door marked CHAPLAIN.

Jack knocked. It was opened by a broad-shouldered man who was around Jack's age. His deep tan made his blue eye even more brilliant.

The other eye was covered with a patch.

After the men shook hands, Jack handed Dan Forsythe a photo of Pinky Ring, "I think we had a run-in with the same guy. What can you tell me about him?"

Dan looked down at the photo, and winced. "Four years ago, I was assigned to Berlin, which is where I ran into this man." He pointed to his collar. "I wasn't wearing this back then. In fact, I was in deep cover, investigating a leak in our security there. I was introduced to him by one of our boys who wasn't feeling appreciated and had an itch to freelance. This man was his handler. He works for some sort of free-lance agency that trolls for soldiers of fortune willing to do exterminations for the organization's clients—mostly rogue terrorist cells, and unfriendly governments."

"How did your meeting go?"

Dan flipped up the eye patch to reveal a pulpy hole.

He shrugged. "When I thought about it afterward, it reminded me of a lamb going to slaughter. They let me play out my spiel, but trust me, they had me pegged. I don't know what you have on this group—the Quorum—but whatever it is, I hope it's more than what they have on us."

If only you knew, Jack thought.

He shook the captain's hand, and took his leave.

The last thing Jack expected was to see Donna, twelve feet in front of him.

He froze.

She was in a pew, kneeling.

Jack thanked God her eyes were closed, in prayer.

When he took a step forward, a floorboard creaked.

Instinctively, she stirred.

Jack leaped into the confessional, closing the door behind him.

Please, don't let her suspect I'm here.

He was on the priest's side, so odds were his prayer would be answered.

He waited five minutes. He heard nothing.

Dead silence.

He was just about to leave when the door on the other side of the confessional opened. Through the scrim between the two booths, he could faintly make out Donna's features.

Oh...hell.

"Forgive me, Father, for I have sinned," she murmured.

"Um...how long since your last confession?" He wasn't Catholic, but he'd heard that in a movie, so he went with it.

She gave a low chuckle. "Hey, I'm not even Catholic but you're the only game in town." She paused. "You see, Father, I feel as if I've lost a big piece of me, somewhere along the way." Her words were barely a whisper. "I guess it's why I'm here."

"I see." He kept his voice at a low register. "Don't feel guilty about having second thoughts. Not everyone is cut out to be an...an—"

"Assassin." She said the word as easily as if she were saying *flower*. "Father, we both know every human has a dark side. We tamp it down. Sometimes we lose." She was choking on her words. "But have I lost the fight, Father? Have I lost my soul? It feels *so good...to know I'm now prepared to avenge Carl.*"

Jack let her sob until finally she was silent. "This urge to avenge your...your loved one—I swear to you, *it isn't healthy.*"

"You're wrong! When I kill, it'll be for Carl. Don't you see? It will be my redemption! Because every mission will put me one step closer to moving on!"

"No, you're wrong!" he hissed. "Others can do it. Others can make them...*make them pay.*"

She shook her head. "Others? What 'other'? No one hurts like I do! No one misses him more than me. No 'other' bore his children, or listens to their sobs at night, when they try to remember him." She wiped her face with her hand. "*But I remember him.*" The iciness in her voice sent a shiver down Jack's back. "So you see, it has to be me. You know it, and I know it. So let's not pretend otherwise."

She was right. There would be no more pretending—on his part, anyway.

She bowed her head. "What is my penance, Father?"

It's not yours to pay, he thought. It's mine.

"Your turmoil isn't going to be solved with a few Hail Marys. Please do some more soul searching. Before it's…too late."

She nodded.

He saw her rise from the bench. The curtain moved, indicating she was out of the booth. He listened for her footstep and then the door shutting behind her.

But of course, it was already too late.

There was nothing left he could do for her but pray.

Or take down the Quorum himself.

The latter was a given, but he knew the former would come into play along the way as well.

TWO YEARS LATER

21

The Hit

A hit is an assassination, pure and simple.

No, take that back: there is nothing pure about killing someone. A hit by any other name—assassination, extermination, liquidation, termination, murder, homicide, slaying, the old F3 (find, fix, and finish)—stains the soul.

And there's nothing simple about killing someone. Properly done, it takes planning, sometimes months at a time. And no matter how many details are presumed covered, there's always some bit of minutiae that isn't considered, only to rear its ugly head when it's time to pull the trigger.

Afterward, the hit man—or woman—is never the same. The emotional scar tissue around the heart grows thicker with each hit.

But the heart is still in there, somewhere.

You just have to be brave enough and persistent enough to find it.

∼

THE PRISONER, A FORMER SERBIAN GENERAL KNOWN BY THE name of Ratko Zoran, insisted on being called doctor, in deference to his pre-war occupation. Jack readily accommodated his request: prior to taking a cattle prod to the good doctor's genitals.

Using the man's professional title and in a respectful tone, he asked for the name of Zoran's Russian contact in the harvesting of human organs from the prisoners under his control during the Bosnian War.

Dr. Zoran's anguished squeals had no effect on Jack. He was willing to bide his time. After all, he'd already elicited the only thing Acme's client, the Yugoslavian government, had asked for—the name of the Swiss bank, which had handled the funds embezzled during Slobodan Miloševićs reign. At this point, any other knowledge the man, known throughout the country as "the Sadistic Serbian Surgeon," was willing to part with was icing atop a pair of black and blue balls.

He was just about to prod Dr. Zoran again when a text came through on his cell phone:

KD down. ID. Sofia B.

The news was depressing. Apparently, an Acme agent, Kiril Dragonov, had been murdered in the neighboring country of Bulgaria. And because Jack was the closest operative, he was in charge of identifying the remains.

For every action, there is an equal and opposite reaction. Kiril—full of life, quick with a joke, and insightful on the matters of human character—was lying on some cold steel slab. On the other hand, Ratko—who had murdered tens of thousands and profited handsomely off the sale of their body parts—might walk away a eunuch, but he'd walk away nonetheless.

Life just wasn't fair.

The cattle prod next landed on Zoran's right cheek. Jack held it there until even he was sick from the stench of searing flesh.

It was in just the right place to nudge a vain man into spilling his guts. The contact's name poured out of him.

So did the promise to reveal other contacts—those in Russia who had provided aid and arms. "But—but please! Not my face again—please! I'm a plastic surgeon, and I've got to look my best!"

"Don't worry about the fucking scar, Doc. Now that you've given up this guy, he'll come looking for you so that he can skin you alive." Jack slid a pad and pen in front of Zoran. "If you come through with the intel, you'll get a new face and a ticket to the United States, courtesy of the State Department's Witness Protection program."

The doctor hesitated before writing. "How do I know you'll honor this promise?"

Jack smacked Zoran's cheek with the cattle prod. "Doctor, one way or another, I'll get the information."

The man pursed his lips. Finally, he nodded.

Jack untied Zoran's restraints and watched as he scribbled furiously on the pad in front of him. What the man didn't know, but Jack did, was that he'd been given authority to make the offer without the use of torture.

In other words, the cattle prod was Jack's idea.

When Zoran was done, Jack took the pad and nodded to

the Yugoslavian guards to take the prisoner away. He'd be held until the intel was verified.

As he headed out the door, Jack turned back to Zoran. "Remember one thing, doctor—they may not find you in your new life, but I'll always know where you are."

The doctor grimaced—not from the pain, but from a problem that would last him a lifetime—Jack.

THE MAN SENT BY BULGARIA'S INTELLIGENCE AGENCY, HPC, TO meet Jack's flight was a bearded hulking giant of a man named Nikolay Krastevich. In broken but serviceable English, he informed Jack that HPC had its own morgue, where Kiril Dragonov's body was being held for identification. Nikolay also assured him that before the webcam footage was deleted, it was downloaded onto a thumb drive, as per Ryan's request.

He tossed it to Jack, who caught it with one hand.

Through the years, Jack had shared missions and beers with Kiril. He would sorely miss his friend, personally and professionally. Like Jack, Kiril had been an excellent sharpshooter. Over the past few months, he had been assigned to follow up on their Eastern European leads related to the Quorum.

Should he meet Kiril's fate one day, he wondered who'd be sent to retrieve his body, and where it would be sent, since there was no place he called home, let alone anyone to mourn him.

Having arrived in the middle of Sofia's rush hour, Jack and Nikolay fought the traffic all the way between the airport and HPC. Jack didn't understand Nikolay's curses, but the hand gestures that went with them were understood in any language.

"You live now in Paris?" Nikolay asked between honks.

So that Nikolay could keep his eyes on the road, Jack resisted the urge to nod instead of talk. "Yes—for now." As if he had anywhere else to go.

Nikolay nodded sagely. "My kind of town. Land of lovers, eh?"

Jack wanted to tell him, *I wouldn't know.*

But that would be a lie. He'd been in love in Paris, once.

He didn't have to answer because Nikolay pulled into the parking lot of the morgue.

Considering Kiril's face had been blown away, there wasn't much to ID, so the process took all of five minutes. It was more of a formality, really, since they'd already identified him from his fingerprints.

Jack asked Nikolay to cremate Kiril's body and have the ashes interred in a local cemetery.

"No family, eh?" Nikolay shook his head as he genuflected.

Jack was silent all the way back to his hotel room.

Someday, the operative sent to ID Jack's body would say the same about him.

THE WEBCAM FOOTAGE SHOWED THAT THE SHOOTER WAS a woman.

Jack turned white when he realized who he was looking at.

But...how could that be? *She was presumed dead.*

He zoomed in to make sure.

But of course, he'd know her anywhere.

When she was done, she strolled away from the car, toward another parked across the street.

He also recognized the man in the driver's seat.

Somehow, they had survived—

Both of them.

Anger surged through him. He slammed his computer shut.

He wondered how Ryan would react when he heard the news. He'd never seen his boss lose his cool, but there was a first time for everything.

JACK THOUGHT IT WOULD BE BEST TO DELIVER THE NEWS TO Ryan in person, but he suggested they meet somewhere outside of Acme headquarters. He didn't want anyone else to know he was in town.

They met in a private hotel suite at one of the large, face-less hotels ringing LAX. When Jack answered Ryan's knock, he shook his hand, but he didn't say anything. So that it was easier for Ryan to see their dilemma with his own eyes, he played the Bulgaria webcam for him.

When it was over, Ryan's face had lost all its color. His hand shook as he clicked the button to play the recording again. And again.

Both men sat quietly for ten minutes. Finally, Ryan said, "Now we know for sure."

"But...how?" Jack could barely speak through his rage.

"Does it matter? No. What's more, we're going to let them think they got away with it," Ryan explained.

Jack shook his head, confused.

"That way, they'll get cocky. They'll make stupid mistakes. They'll come into the light." Ryan paced the room as he tried to think it through.

"I go solo on this one." Jack was adamant.

"You'll get no argument from me on that," Ryan assured him. "You're naked on this mission for as long as you see fit. In fact, you report only to me on your progress, and in person. We can't take the chance that there's a leak within Acme. When you feel you need back-up, you let me know. We'll put together an airtight support team."

They shook on it.

It would have to be a crackerjack team—focused, with no hidden agendas. Considering the damage done to Acme— and personally, to Donna and her family—the mission deserved nothing less.

All the more reason Donna would have to sit this one out. Revenge was not the issue.

This was about redemption.

Thank goodness Ryan saw it this way, too.

Now, it was time for Jack to set the trap.

RIGHT NOW

22

Unavoidably Detained

Tally of This Year's "Undercover Lover" Award:

3rd Runner Up, with 6% of the Vote: Aleksandr Loris-Melikov Moscow Bureau. Cover Occupation: Caviar Exporter What Makes Him Memorable: Aleksandr claims that the Siberian gulag prisoner number, tattooed on his bulging right bicep (259.08), equals the size of his cock, in millimeters. (Yes, this has been confirmed.)

2nd Runner Up, with 12% of the Vote: Alberto Francisco Sanchez Rubio Barcelona Bureau. Cover Occupation: Toreador What Makes Him Memorable: Most Audacious Pick-Up Line: If I show you where I've been gored, will you kiss it and make it better?"

1st Runner Up, with 39% of the Vote: Dominic Fleming, 12th Baron of Wellesington London Bureau. Cover Occupation: "I dabble." What Makes Him Memorable: His "physical stamina" —

and the fact that afterwards he serves a perfect British tea with the most heavenly scones!

Winner, with 41% of the Vote: Jack Craig Paris Bureau. Cover Occupation: International Banker What Makes Him Memorable: Everything! You're drawn to him because of the sadness in his eyes. Should he take you as a lover, you'll discover he's both fierce and gentle. But don't fall in love with him, because he makes no promises.

THERE WERE NO DIRECT FLIGHTS FROM SOFIA TO ANY AIRPORT IN the United States, Acme's in-house travel coordinator explained to Jack. She'd have to route him through Frankfurt or London's Heathrow.

"Fine, no problem," he assured her. "Listen, do me a favor, sweetheart. So that I won't be disturbed on either flight, put me up in a first-class seat—oh, and get the seat adjacent so I can avoid prying eyes while I work."

"Sure, anything for this year's Undie winner," she gushed.

"Um…thanks."

"You know, I voted for you."

"You didn't really have to."

"Oh, but I did! You're the only one I haven't slept with." Her voice was filled with the promise to make it worth his while, should he want to rectify the matter.

"You're out of Acme Manhattan, am I right?"

"You've got that right," she purred. "Maybe that's where I should schedule your stopover."

"No, don't bother. I've reached my quota with that office."

He meant it as a joke, but by the clipped, frigid tone of her voice, he realized she didn't find it funny as she told him, "You can pick up your ticket upon check-in."

"Which airline?"

"Which is your favorite?"

"Lufthansa, if it can be arranged. If not, I'll take British Air."

He heard the tap, tap, tap of her fingers on a keyboard. "So sorry, but it seems the only seats available are on Bulgaria Air, you can transfer at Heathrow to British Air."

Ah, he thought, payback time. "Then I guess that will have to do."

Her goodbye was a dial tone.

When he got to the gate, he learned his ticket was a middle seat in coach, on a full flight.

The ticket sleeve held a digital photo of his travel coordinator. She could have easily made Maxim's Top Ten list of Hottest Women.

Maybe I need to loosen up, he chided himself.

One thing was for sure—she'd vote for someone else next time.

Good. It was one title he'd happily surrender.

JACK WONDERED IF THE TRAVEL COORDINATOR ROUTED HIM through London because she knew a snowstorm was about to hit the British Isles.

The plane rocked and rolled during landing. When he

asked the coordinator to book him a hotel accommodation near Heathrow, she clicked her tongue in mock sympathy. "Sorry, Mr. Craig, but there's nothing available. I'm sure there's a spare bench there at Heathrow to accommodate your big, strapping frame...Oh, there isn't? Let me check the rest of the city. There may not be any taxis running, but you can catch the Underground's Piccadilly Line, which takes you right into the heart of the city."

"May I speak to Ryan, please?" Jack tried to keep his tone nice and easy.

A moment later, Ryan's voice came on the line. "Dominic is expecting your call."

Jack groaned, then hung up.

The last thing he wanted to do was rendezvous with Acme's London bureau agent, Dominic Fleming.

In previous dealings with the British agent, he'd come to two conclusions—the first being that the man was a blowhard, and the second, that it was wise to take everything he said with a grain of salt large enough to choke a racehorse.

The only thing that mitigated Ryan's mandate was that the Brit was a charter member of several of London's top private clubs, including Annabel's, the Groucho, and Soho House. Invariably, he arranged for a few comely ladies to accompany them.

"Let's meet at the Groucho, old boy." Dominic's lilting baritone promised fun and games. "In fact, I bequeath you first dibs on my other guests! I met them while perusing the latest shipment of bondage accouterments in 50 & Dean. Buttercup and Delilah are fetish models, and all that it implies: lush figures, nimble bodies, and compliant enough to prove it in the two boudoir suites I've reserved for us at the club."

Jack laughed. "You're on—but only if you promise not to interrogate my playmate afterward, as to the highlights of my bedside manner. This obsession you have with the Undies is ruining our bromance."

For the past five years, Jack had edged out the handsomely square-jawed blond aristocrat for the "Undercover Lover" award, an unofficial poll run by Spooklandia's worldwide network of female desk operatives. Dominic had made it no secret that he was pulling out all stops to best Jack in the next Undies, as it was euphemistically called.

"Not to worry," Dominic assured him. "I can easily access the Groucho's security feed and analyze your technique for myself. This gives me the added advantage of being spared your conquest's rapturous recital—which, by what confessions I've heard thus far, have more to do with your dark, brooding demeanor than any super-human prowess."

Since Donna's transformation, he'd done everything—make that, everyone—he could, to forget her. He'd lost count of the number of women he'd bedded. On purpose, there was no pattern to the partners he chose. They came in all shapes and sizes. One day, she may be a blonde, the next day a brunette, perhaps followed by a redhead even later the same night. Their temperament varied, too. A flirt might presume she'd said all the right things to get him up to her flat. In truth, a shy woman who was awed by his attention was just as likely to attract him. And he'd just as soon fuck a nurse or a waitress as a lawyer—or a prostitute, for that matter.

If they were ready, willing and able, married women weren't a problem for him—unless were stay-at-home mothers, for obvious reasons.

"Perhaps if I tamped down my naturally sunny disposition," Dominic suddenly added after Jack's long pause.

"That would be a start. You may also want to cut back on all the in-the-act selfies. Most women prefer you to share the moment of ecstasy with them alone, as opposed to your growing legion of Facebook fans."

It was a shot in the dark, but Jack knew he'd hit a bull's eye when Dominic muttered dryly, "Let me point out that anyone can claim, 'Washington slept here.' I'm providing them historical proof, the ungrateful trollops! Yes, well, to that end, here's to burnishing our reputations—and theirs, later tonight. Nine sharp."

JACK WOULD HAVE BEEN ON TIME, TOO, HAD HE NOT recognized the man walking out of the Groucho Club's double front door, just as he was walking into it:

The man with the pinky ring.

Their eyes met only for a split second, but that was enough time for Pinky Ring to realize that Jack had no intention of losing him this time.

Pinky Ring slammed the door on Jack's knee and ran down the street. Jack hobbled after him, down Dean Street. But when the man turned left on Bouchier, Jack realized there was no way to catch him on foot.

The hack, which had just let Pinky Ring out, had been stopped at the light at the other end of the block, while turning onto Old Compton street. Jack opened the driver-side door and tossed the cabbie out of the cab.

But instead of following Pinky Ring, Jack headed in the opposite direction—toward Old Compton, then right onto Wardour. Bouchier dead-ended on Wardour Street, and he guessed—rightly so—that Pinky Ring would turn left, back toward Old Compton, where it would be easier for him to catch another cab.

When Pinky Ring waved him down, Jack pulled over, skidding in front of another cab to do so. The competing cabbie rewarded him with a two-finger salute before screeching off.

Pinky Ring opened the door and was about to hop in when he saw Jack's face in the review mirror. Jack grabbed at his coat sleeve, but the man jerked away and fell back—

Right into the path of a double-decker bus.

The driver tried to swerve to miss Pinky Ring, but he still winged him. The Mercedes finished the job the bus started. It smacked into him, then dragged him half a block down the street before swerving away.

Jack pushed his way through the crowd until he could kneel over him. The front of Pinky Ring's shirt was already soaked in the crimson blood.

No matter how hard Jack begged the dying man to explain his connection to Carl, Pinky Ring's whispers were lost in the din of the shocked throng as his life flickered out.

Cradling him gave Jack the opportunity to pick the dying man's coat pocket. As he'd hoped, the man's wallet was there, as was a door key.

He also twisted off the man's ring and slipped it onto his own finger before lurching off into the thickening crowd.

By the time he made it back to the Groucho, Dominic had, as the concierge so delicately put it, "retired with his other guests." The man eyed Jack knowingly. He turned in order to pull a brass door key, embossed with the number 13.

He had a new lucky number.

Jack took the key. As he suspected, when he got to his room, Dominic had one of his other guests waiting for him there.

In a breathless whisper, she exclaimed," Why, hello! My name is Delilah, and I've been very, very naughty!" She pointed to the whip at the foot of the bed.

As ready, willing and able as she obviously was to assume the position of a chastened waif, he sent her down the hall, to Dominic's room.

He was glad he did not share a wall with his friend. Tonight, he needed his sleep.

Tomorrow, the battle against the Quorum would begin in earnest.

23

Disciplinary Actions

*Case File #415516-P, on the Extermination of Franz Stein, a.k.a.,
Frankie "The Monster" Stein, a.k.a, "Frankenstein" (the
preferred nickname of those who are closest to him), and the
titular head of California's most active neo-Nazi terror cell,
"Nazis for the Ultimate Terror of Society" (or NUTS for short,
no pun intended):*

Filing Agent: Donna Stone
*The target entered the Lodi, California 24-Hour De-Lish
Donut Shoppe at 02:14, a locale, which he openly frequented in
the early morning hours, and in which I had secured an
undercover position.*

*At the time, I was the only one behind the counter. The other
waitress who is usually on the overnight shift wasn't feeling too
well and went home early. (Okay, yeah, thanks to the few drops of
Visine I'd put in her iced tea.)*

*Frankenstein was always a big flirt with whoever was behind
the counter, but that night, I made it extra easy for him to turn*

on the charm. In other words, I dimpled up, batted my eyelashes, and thrust Pixie and Dixie practically in his face.

Needless to say, he was smitten.

There was just enough hanky-panky for me to spike his dirty hippy. (Note to Ryan: Cross my heart and hope to die, this does not, repeat, does not refer to any pal he may have had along, but is in fact the nickname of his drink of choice, a Chai tea with a shot of espresso, and therefore no provocation for an unauthorized hit.) As hoped, the diuretic had him running to the little boy's room, allowing me enough time to check the text messages on his iPhone, which he'd left on the counter. (His cell's case is adorned with skull-and-crossbones. Why am I not surprised?)

The location of the meet with the Russian arms dealer, Yuri Petrovich, was in fact verified.

Unfortunately, the suspect reappeared just at this moment.

Okay, I'll admit it—all hell broke loose.

Since you're reading this, you can guess who drove away on a brand new Harley Street Bob.

(Well, I had to make it look like he was killed for something, didn't I? Can I keep it? Please? Pretty please, with sugar on top? JUST KIDDING.)

Unfortunately, in my haste to leave the kill zone, I left Frankenstein's iPhone on the counter. I left no prints, but I'm pretty certain the phone was open to the text about the meet-and-greet with Yuri.

When his next-of-kin (cough! Fellow skinheads) collect his belongings, do you think they'll have his cell's security code? Hope not. I'd hate for that little party to be called off, since the mission directive is to be there for the arms exchange, and the sanctioned extermination of Yuri.

D. Stone

[AGENT DISCIPLINARY REPORT, IN REFERENCE TO CASE FILE #415516-P]

Agent Stone was successful in the extermination, as well as in gathering intel about the upcoming rendezvous between NUTS and a known Russian arms dealer.

Despite this, while her asides are quite colorful and entertaining in their nature, it has been strongly requested (yet again) that she forego any unnecessary declarations that may compromise Acme's ability to protect itself and its clients from political and/or legal complications.

As for the reference made to the potentially illegal confiscation of the target's means of transportation, for the record, the property referenced above ("Harley Street Bob") is now in the hands of local law enforcement.

Ryan Clancy, Director, Acme Corporation

FILE NOTATION

To: Ryan Clancy, Director, Acme Corporation
From: Jack Craig, Mission Leader, Project Quorum
Told you she'd be trouble!

Jack

PS: You owe me that Benjamin.

"WE'VE GOT NOTHING," ARNIE DECLARED AS HE TOSSED PINKY Ring's dossier in front of Jack and Ryan. "His IDs are all fake. I broke the security code on his cell phone, but a lot of good that did us. It had a kill button, on a timer. When he didn't respond with the right code within an hour, that damn thing fried its memory card."

Jack shook his head. "Bullshit. There's got to be something."

Arnie shrugged. "Okay, yeah, there's something. But nothing legit. The room key belongs to a suite in Claridge's. He checked in under an assumed name. He was careful to leave no prints in the room, not even on the toilet seat. I found a couple of pubic hairs and sent them over to Interpol to see if they can do a DNA trace."

"Good luck with that," Jack muttered. "They may not have even been his."

Ryan raised a brow. "Is that a knock against the hotel's cleaning staff?"

Without thinking, Jack tossed the dead man's ring with one hand, only to catch it in the fist of his other one. "Pinky Ring could have made up for the fact that he wasn't a lady's man by buying a playmate or two. If you found three strands of hair, they could well belong to three different women."

"Too much information," Emma muttered as she clicked away furiously on her computer. Suddenly she gave a long, low whistle. "Hello, Kitty! I have a facial recognition match on his morgue picture with an old photo from East Germany. He was a Stasi colonel who disappeared after the country's reunification with West Germany."

"Way to go, new girl." Jack grinned at Emma. She ducked her head, but not before he saw her whole face go red.

Seeing Arnie frown, Jack coughed through a chuckle. The dude needs to grow a pair and ask her out, he thought to himself.

"One more ghost the War Crimes Commission can put to rest," Ryan muttered.

"Tap into London's Ring of Steel," Jack suggested. "Scan the surveillance feed at Claridge's, for his check-in date. That way, we'll be able to trace his path since he arrived in London, and from where." He tossed the ring up in the air again. "We can also see where else he's been since his arrival in London. Maybe it will lead us to information on the stolen microdot."

"Jeez, Jack! You were right! The hairs came from three different women!"

Jack was joking when he made the assumption. Hearing he'd been right was reason to pause. He forgot about the ring to stare at what Arnie had pulled up on his computer screen.

When the ring came down, it hit the table with a loud clack—

Then landed on the carpeted floor with a dull thud.

The crest popped off, revealing a tiny cell phone memory card.

Everyone stared down at it.

"Bingo," Jack murmured. He scooped up the memory card and handed it to Arnie. "Care to do the honors?"

Arnie popped it into Pinky Ring's phone, replacing the fried memory card. While he crossed the fingers of one hand, he entered the security code with the other.

He hooted when the phone's security wall disappeared.

Quickly, he downloaded the phone's contact directory, and its text messages.

Arnie clicked onto the phone's photo scroll. A digital photo appeared. "He has a picture of the Hollywood sign, here in LA." Despite swiping the screen a few times, the photo stayed put. Arnie frowned. "Seems it's the only picture he's taken."

"Let me see." Jack stood over his shoulder to scrutinize the screen. "It's stock photography. I've seen that same shot in a million ads."

Arnie's eyes got big. "It is, but it isn't. See this?" He pointed to the second O on the Hollywood sign. "If you look closely, you'll see that it looks a bit wavy, somewhat out of focus. There's a message buried within this image."

Emma rolled her chair close to Arnie's so she could see the screen, too. "Wow! You mean, some sort of steganography?"

Arnie nodded and turned to Ryan. "I'll need to decode it. If cipher text is involved, it'll go faster with Emma's help."

Ryan shrugged. "Get on it, you two." He noticed Jack stifling a yawn. "You came straight over from London, so I presume you've been up more than twenty-four hours. This may take an hour or so. If you need to grab some shut-eye, feel free to go back to your apartment."

Jack shook his head. "The moment I do, you'll call me

back here. Arnie's pretty quick. I'll just grab an empty cubicle or something."

He spoke too soon. Acme's offices were buzzing, a veritable hive of nervous activity. Every cubicle held a desk operative, furtively murmuring into a headset to some agent out in the field, perhaps in peril.

Then he remembered the rooftop garden.

It was a smart move on Ryan's part, setting up a quiet space where an Acme employee could go—if only for a few minutes, to take a breath of fresh air under the perennially turquoise sky as they gazed down onto the broad boulevard below, where normal people strolled by, going about their average, uneventful days—before crashing back into the reality of a very dangerous world.

He slipped out the fire exit, taking the steps two at a time.

The bench he chose was flanked by a box hedge on three sides, and faced the ocean.

He stared out at it for maybe a moment, before he fell fast asleep.

JACK AWOKE TO THE SOUND OF HER LAUGH.

He opened one eye and glanced around, just to make sure he wasn't still dreaming—about her, in fact, as was sometimes the case, more often than he liked to admit.

"Yeah, Ryan, I get it. When I rode off on the bike, I went too far." Her tone was anything but contrite. In fact, it was downright playful.

"Donna, you need to take this seriously! It could have

blown the mission wide open." Jack could hear Ryan pacing across the rooftop's flagstone patio. "The skinheads are out for blood. The Lodi police are dragging the river, searching for the body of one 'Doreen Sugarbaker,' a.k.a, your alias, and the doughnut shop was left in a shambles!" He stopped to catch his breath. "To top it off, you stole the target's Harley—for a goddamn joyride!"

"Sure, why not? It's one sweet Harley—twin cam 96, six-speed cruise drive. Can you imagine popping a wheelie on that thing? I couldn't do it. I'm just a slip of a girl." She paused then added with a seductive drawl, "Come on, admit it—when you saw me pull up on it at the rendezvous site, weren't you tempted to give it a try? I mean, after those couple of years you spent undercover with the Aryan Nation—"

"How the hell did you know about that?" Jack had never heard Ryan lose his cool until just that moment.

She snickered. "Whoa, don't get your tighty-whities in a wad! You know what they say: 'Dossiers are meant to be read.'"

"I don't have a dossier!"

"Of course you don't," she agreed sweetly. "At least, not here at Acme. But the one the CIA has on you is, oh my gawd, humongous! Remember last summer, when you introduced me to your buddy who runs the CIA's National Clandestine Service? Well, let me put it this way—the dude can't hold his tequila. All it took was a little Truth or Dare, and presto! Your file miraculously appeared on his computer screen."

"Donna Stone, whenever you pull stunts like these, I

regret the day I hired you." Jack could only imagine Ryan seething through clenched teeth.

"If it's any consolation, my dare was a lot worse. I had to swallow the worm at the bottom of the bottle." She giggled. "Ryan, seriously, if you keep frowning like that, no amount of Botox will get rid of those creases on your forehead."

Dead silence.

"I'm sorry, boss. Truly I am." Her words were weighted with sadness. "Not just for snooping into your file, but for breaking protocol with Frankenstein, too. I guess I felt so... oh, I don't know—alive after that encounter! One moment he's got his hands around my throat and I could feel the air leaving my body. All I could think about was how many people he's killed or hurt, and how many more would die, if I didn't stop him. Then the next thing I know, I'm stabbing him in the jugular with a steak knife." She paused. "Hey don't give me that look. It's not as if he didn't deserve it."

"I have half a mind to take you off this mission, Donna. You're a loose cannon, and I can't afford that."

"But you won't, because the arms purchase between Yuri and the skinheads goes down tomorrow, and you don't have time to bring in another assassin, let alone one who looks as great as me in a tight skirt and a push-up bra."

There was a long pause as Ryan faced the reality she'd just laid out.

Suddenly, she laughed, "But hey, it's not like I pulled a Jack Craig, or anything."

What the hell does that mean? Jack wondered. Is she saying I'm some sort of a lone wolf—a wild card? My God, I'm not an emotional train wreck! She is!

All of a sudden, he regretted not making a stronger case against Ryan hiring her.

He certainly regretted he'd ever felt sorry for her.

Most of all, he hated the fact he'd fallen in love with her.

Well, now that he knew what she thought of him, he'd certainly stay far away from the lovely, but lethal, Mrs. Stone.

"In fact, Donna, what you did is exactly something Jack would do—and I did exactly to you what I'd do to him under the same circumstances. I've put a disciplinary report in the mission file."

"But—but I've got two of those already this year! A third one means I'll be docked my year-end bonus!"

"You should have thought about that before you took your little joyride," Ryan growled. "You're lucky you're so good at what you do. And by that, I don't mean baking pies."

"Speaking of which, I'll be baking some, right after the mission. I'll be sure to save one for you."

"Yeah, okay, whatever—but the disciplinary report stays in the file."

She laughed. "We'll see. It's your favorite—cherry." From the click of her heels on the flagstone, Jack could tell she was walking away.

She's got him wrapped around her finger, Jack thought. He shook his head and rubbed his tired eyes as he contemplated the real Donna Stone, as opposed to the one who existed in his fantasies.

The real Donna was so obviously angry. And damaged. And still in mourning for Carl.

He opened his eyes to find Ryan scowling down at him. "Enjoy the entertainment?"

"I didn't mean to eavesdrop," Jack explained. "I came up here to catch a few rays along with some shut-eye."

Ryan waved away the excuse. "She's a pistol, that one."

Jack snorted. "Don't say I didn't warn you. Speaking of which, if my memory serves me right, it's your turn to pay up. "

Ryan acknowledged the declaration with a nod. "What can I say? She's fearless. Twenty-eight executive actions in four years, and most were in hostile environments. She's motivated—"

"For all the wrong reasons," Jack broke in. "Admit it, Ryan."

"You're right. But the reasons don't really matter, as long as she does the job." He glanced up as a plane droned above them, arching out over the Pacific as it ascended from LAX. "Great news! Arnie cracked the cipher in the photo. From all indications, the Quorum is planning something big—here, in LA. As you know, we've been expecting some kind of domestic disturbance for at least a few months, what with all the chatter we've been picking up. Now that we know where, we'll need all hands on deck. By the way, I think it's time you formally meet Donna."

Jack's heart leaped in his chest. As nonchalantly as he could, he muttered, "Sure, whatever works."

"I'm glad to hear you say that. Because I'd like you to go deep cover."

"Where?"

"I just told you—here, in LA—"

Jack let that sink in. It would be difficult, being based in the same town as her. But if he played his cards right, he could keep out of her way.

"—As Carl Stone. You're the right height and build. And the right coloring. In any event, there are no known photos of him."

Jack's eyes went wide. He shook his head. "Wait…what? No, Ryan! Bad idea. *Very, very bad idea*. She's…she's not ready for that!"

"She'll have to be, if we're to smoke out the Quorum. In the meantime, we'll keep her on a need-to-know basis. Whatever they think she has, they want it badly enough to plant a cell or two, specifically in Hilldale."

"I've combed through that place on my hands and knees. Whatever it is, it ain't there, trust me."

"Even if it's not, if it looks as if Carl is back, they'll come calling. That's reason enough for you to take on his identity."

"And all the more reason why she won't want me around. She's got children, remember?"

"I say you're wrong. More than anyone else, she wants the Quorum dead and buried—despite what she learns because of it."

"She doesn't want it any more than I do."

"Yes, with good reason." Ryan didn't have to say it:

Because of Jack, the Quorum knew too much already.

All the more reason they had to find the microdot before it fell into the wrong hands.

If Kiril's murder proved anything, the Quorum was the strongest and the smartest adversary Acme had faced to date.

Jack sighed. "Okay, I'll do it—but only if you're ordering me to do so."

"I am." Ryan rewarded him with a faint grimace that always passed for a smile. "Not that I look forward to breaking the news to her. I'll hold off a day or two until after the arms sales mission. In the meantime, you can close up shop in Paris."

"Sure." Jack couldn't help but laugh at the irony of it all. "I'll stick with my bet that she'll refuse to go along with it."

"You're on."

"After what I've overheard today regarding the ornery Mrs. Stone, you already owe me a hundred bucks. Here's hoping you don't go two-for-two. I'd hate to lose my head over it."

Ryan contemplated that with one eye closed. "Trust me, she'd aim much lower than that."

Jack had no doubt he was right.

24

Swallow

In espionage, a swallow is a female agent who seduces a target in order to coerce or steal intelligence. Sometimes a swallow kills in the line of duty.

The upside is that you get to primp, wear beautiful clothes, and travel on someone else's dime.

The downside is when blood gets on your Jimmy Choos.

Best-case scenario: the blood is not your own.

[EXCERPT FROM THE FIRST ENTRY IN DONNA STONE'S PERSONAL handbook]

Here's my to-do list:

- *First, stall on sex with Yuri Petrovich, until the skinheads show up. Done.*
- *Next, plant a GPS system on one of the skinheads, so*

*that ATF can track and apprehend them during the
pick-up. Check.*

- *And finally, as a show of tit-for-tat diplomacy with
Uncle Sam's publicly acknowledged BFF, Russia, I'm to
see to it that Yuri never leaves his hotel room alive.*

All in good time, dearie. All in good time.

*In fact, all of this is supposed to be accomplished before three
o'clock, the time at which I have to pick up my ten-year-old, Jeff,
and a carload of his teammates for an after-school baseball game.
Otherwise I'll have to face the wrath of two other mothers for
having blown the team's shot at taking the county title without a
playoff game —*

*I pray that the 405 isn't a nightmarish backup by the time I
head home.*

THE WEBCAM FEED ON DONNA STONE'S HOUSE CAME IN
beautifully on the dashboard monitor on Jack's spanking
new blood-red Lamborghini roadster.

Hell, if he was going to be stuck in this suburgatory, at
the very least Acme could pony up for a lease on a real car.
Ryan frowned, but he signed the paperwork nonetheless.

Over the past few years, Jack had forced himself to avoid
any news of her. But this was something nearly impossible
to do. On the spook loops, where she was referred to as
@WifeyAssassin, she was building quite a reputation as a
killing machine, what with the extraordinary number of
exterminations and her ingenuity in tracking her targets.

For the past hour—immediately after making a cherry

pie, from scratch no less—he watched as Donna scribbled away in a notebook. Was it a recipe book? If so, when had she started this little hobby? As soon as she left the house, he'd have to check into it, to make sure she wasn't breaking protocol yet again. Ryan would flip out if he found out she was memorializing her missions.

While writing, she'd been fiddling with something—an antique locket on a chain, from the look of it. What was the significance? he wondered.

Right on time, the call came to Donna's cell phone. Since he'd tapped her phone, he also heard the message: "Yesterday you reserved a copy of *The Last Tycoon*. It's now waiting for you at the front desk."

Jack tensed up. Show time, he thought.

In truth, the call came from an Acme operative—Marion, a Hilldale librarian—informing Donna of an intel drop from her handler, Abu Nagashahi. On the way home, Donna and her children would stop for an ice pop, from the truck driven by Abu. He'd hand her a particular pop, encoded with her mission—stop the Quorum from whatever they had planned for the fair city of LA.

And partnering with Jack.

He also wondered how she'd break the news to the kids that Daddy was finally home.

Well, he'd soon find out.

Hurriedly, Donna closed the notebook. She took it and the locket back to the curio cabinet from where she'd taken them and locked the cabinet before rushing up the stairs.

When she came back down, she had Trisha in her arms. The little girl rubbed the sleep from her eyes with one hand, but clung tightly to Donna with the other as her mother dipped to grab her purse and keys from the lowboy in the entry foyer.

Donna had just flung open the front door when something stopped her cold. Her nose went up in the air, as if she'd smelled something that didn't agree with her. She let loose with an expletive before rushing into the kitchen.

So that he could follow her, Jack switched the monitor to the one he'd hidden in her kitchen so many years ago, when he and Arnie were investigating Carl's death. What he saw made him chuckle:

The oven was smoking.

She plopped Trisha onto the kitchen banquette before reaching for the oven door handle—

Burning her hand in the process.

Frantically, she scanned the kitchen until she found what she was looking for—an oven mitt. It was tucked under Lassie's head. The dog, half-asleep by the front door, yipped as Donna yanked the mitt away.

A second later, she scooped the pie out of the oven and slammed it on the marble countertop. The crust was singed black.

Shaking her head angrily, she scooped Trisha back into her arms, along with her bag and keys and headed out the garage door with Lassie at her heels.

She drove away so fast that she didn't even notice the red Lamborghini, parked a half-block from the house on the other side of the street.

Jack waited a few minutes after Donna's minivan had disappeared around the corner, then checked to make sure the street was empty before leaving his car and heading to the house.

Once inside, his first stop was the curio cabinet. Yes, there it was, her notebook—

Make that her cookbook. The binder was embossed *Favorite Recipes*. With a black magic marker, she'd scrawled in her girlishly circular handwriting:

Personal

Halfheartedly he picked up the book, but the thought of flipping through it made him wince. Maybe her little housewife's hobby was good anger management therapy. It certainly paid off in one way—the woman could sure cook! He knew, because sometimes he sampled her leftovers.

Too bad about the cherry pie, he thought.

He was just about to open the notebook when he saw the locket. He picked it up. It was definitely an antique—heart-shaped with intricately embossed sterling silver, hanging on a delicate chain.

He nudged the clasp open with his thumb.

Inside was a picture of Carl on one side.

Yes, he thought, she still loves him deeply.

If she was working through the tangled mix of emotion by writing down her thoughts, so be it. It wasn't his business, or Acme's. Hell, hadn't they done enough to the poor woman? Acme had stolen everything from her: the life she once had. Her innocence. Her happiness.

Her husband.

Her Carl no longer existed.

He hoped that, someday, she could find it in herself to forgive him for that.

He put the notebook back in the bottom of the curio case and locked it.

PHYSICALLY, THE CHILDREN HAD GROWN BY LEAPS AND BOUNDS —at least from what he could tell in the pictures of them with their mother posted on the bulletin boards over their bedroom desks and on their bedside tables.

A quick glance through her closet confirmed she was still a size 4 gown. In the air, there was the slightest whisper of Pure Poison by Dior, her killer scent.

The lady had quite a sense of humor.

By now, she would have received the mission missive, informing her that he'd be posing as Carl. In case Ryan was wrong about her—what did he call it? Oh yeah, "team spirit"—Jack would be sure to prepare himself for a frosty welcome.

He looked down at his feet. The last thing he needed was for her to be pissed because he was also tracking mud all over the place. From what he remembered about her afternoon schedule, rounding up the children from their after-school activities and rendezvousing with Abu might actually leave him enough time for a quick shower.

All the towels in the bathroom closet were pink.

So were the disposable razors. The only shaving cream came in a pink can, too.

Jack squirted a little into the palm of his hand. It smelled of lavender, ginger, and vanilla.

He groaned. It would be like shaving with cake icing.

Too bad, he'd have to make do.

DONNA STONE COULD USE A MAN AROUND THE HOUSE, HE thought. Or at least a new water heater.

He'd been standing under the fancy new showerhead for just fifteen minutes, and in that time, the water pounding down on him had gone from almost scalding—the way he liked it—to downright tepid.

I wonder how she'll take the suggestion to spring for a new hot water heater. I guess it depends on how well she responded to the news of my role in this mission. If, after all these years, she's still angry over Carl's disappearance, she may tell me to stick this bar of soap where the sun don't shine.

Then again, maybe it had been long enough that she was ready for a new mister in her life. Even honeypots like to snuggle up to a warm body, every now and then.

Especially after the adrenaline rush of a hit.

He'd bedded enough of them to know this firsthand.

He got a hard-on thinking about her body next to his, there, in the shower.

In the white four-poster bed, not twenty feet away.

He'd take her on the floral-patterned chaise lounge, if she'd let him.

Suddenly, he was ashamed of himself. He had reduced her to that: another conquest.

Just because Donna Stone was an assassin.

For a moment there, he'd forgotten why she'd become one.

Forget sex, let alone love. She lived for one thing only: revenge.

AH, HELL, THEY'RE HOME. ALREADY? WHAT THE —

Damn it, they're right here, in the bedroom!

He'd let his guard down—in fact, he was humming as he shaved.

But a sixth sense warned him that he wasn't alone.

The door was open, just a crack. Through it, he saw the little one: Trisha. Her eyes were open wide, in awe.

His instinct was to smile at her, to wave, to promise her she had nothing to fear from him.

But before he could do so, Donna was there, too, and Mary and Jeff. Jack had never seen such a look on Donna's face. Gone was the cold calculation, the wariness.

In its place was fear.

She scooped up Trisha and shoved her into Mary's arms. She whispered so softly that he couldn't hear what she was saying. No matter: they'd frozen, like statues, staring at him.

On the other hand, Mary, Jeff, and Trisha looked fascinated.

Make that hopeful.

He took a deep breath and thought, Okay, show time.

WHEN JACK TURNED ON THE CHARM, SERIOUSLY, WHAT WAS NOT to love?

He came out with one towel wrapped around his waist and patting down his damp hair with another, as if he didn't have a care in the world.

As if seeing them all there was the most natural thing in the world.

He was all smiles. That way, the kids could see he was harmless.

He looked Donna straight in the eye as he murmured, "Honey, I'm home," casually, as if they'd seen each other just this morning.

By now, she should have lost her wary stare. She should have fallen into her role in Acme's grand scheme.

Instead, her eyes narrowed.

If looks could kill, he'd have dropped dead, right then and there.

What the hell was wrong with her?

Okay, so be it. She was still pissed at Ryan. He'd carry the show on his own.

First he bent down, so that he was nose-to-nose with Trisha. "Ah, so this is Trisha! My God, you're the sweetest littlest princess in the world! Give me a big, big hug."

The little girl gave him a shy pat on the shoulder, but when he rewarded her with a smile. She practically jumped into his arms. "Yes, that's my girl!"

Seeing her brother move one step closer to him, Jack added, "And Jeff! Wow, boy, how about a handshake, huh?" Jack held out his hand.

The boy took it. When their eyes met, Jeff's wariness melted away under his awed, approving gaze. He pumped Jack's hand desperately, as if he never wanted to let go.

Jack was touched by the boy's show of emotion. Still, so that he didn't embarrass either of them, he made light of it. "You're quite a bruiser, eh, kid?"

And then it was Mary's turn:

Mary, who he knew to be the most jaded—and yes, the most traumatized of all Donna's children.

I can't blow this, he vowed. Otherwise, this mission dies, right here and right now.

We'll never again have a chance like this to end the Quorum.

He started with a smile: one filled with adoration. He followed it up with a real hug—one he hoped would make her think, *he really missed me. He really loves me.*

He's really Dad.

She shivered slightly under his pat. Still, he persisted, albeit more gently, as if she were a fragile piece of china that might break if he wasn't careful...

"Ah, Mary," he murmured softly. "You beautiful little heartbreaker, you–"

But none of this takes her in. Instead, she looked over at her mother, as if to ask, *what now?*

Donna stood there, speechless. Emotions flickered behind her eyes.

She's going to blow it, he thought.

To hell with that.

A second later, he was at her side. Before she could react, he took her in his arms. His lips brushed over hers, gently. Instinctively, she tried to pull back.

But he wouldn't let her.

His kiss stopped her.

It took a moment for her mouth to soften, for her lips to sweeten.

As the kiss deepened with their mutual desire, his mind formed one word:

Perfect.

Suddenly, Jeff and Trisha and Mary were wrapping them

tightly, in a group hug. He could only guess what they were thinking:

Finally, Dad is come home.

He'd forgotten the kids were in the room. Apparently Donna had too, because when she looked down at their bowed heads, her eyes misted over with wistfulness.

It almost broke his heart.

They stayed suspended in the clinch for what seemed like forever.

Then, one by one, the children broke away. Mary, her face a kaleidoscope of emotions, was the first. The others followed suit, slowly, as if they were sleepwalking.

The door closed silently behind them.

That...wasn't so bad, Jack thought.

Hell, who did he think he was he fooling? *It was wonderful.*

Especially the kiss.

Donna must have thought so, too, because she rewarded him with a naughty smile that promised so much.

Well, what do you know? Ha! This is going to be easier than I thought.

He realized how wrong he was when, a second later, she kicked him in his solar plexus. He landed face-down on the carpet, gasping for air.

His pain was doubled when, a second later, she wrenched his arm behind his back, then straight up and out.

"So tell me, you audacious son of a bitch," she growled in his ear, "Who are you, and what the hell do you think you're doing?"

Right then, at that very second, he knew he'd love her for the rest of his life.

Even if it took the rest of his life to convince her he was worthy of it.

But first things first: the Quorum would have to be stopped before it blew up Los Angeles.

Donna and Jack would do it together.

Then they'd get on with the rest of their lives.

Mrs. Stone, I think this is the beginning of a beautiful relationship.

—*THE END*—

Next Up for Donna!

The Housewife Assassin's Greatest Hits (Book 16)

As housewife assassin Donna Stone Craig's life hangs in the balance, a deadly bet with the Grim Reaper brings forth a cavalcade of ghosts from her past: those whom she loved and lost, and those whose lives she took. Their sometimes chilling but always insightful points-of-view on Donna's life leave her with a few regrets, and at the same time grant her the redemption she needs to keep living. But first she must beat the Reaper at his own game.

Other Books by Josie Brown

The True Hollywood Lies Series
Hollywood Hunk
Hollywood Whore

The Totlandia Series
The Onesies - Book 1 (Fall)
The Onesies - Book 2 (Winter)
The Onesies - Book 3 (Spring)
The Onesies - Book 4 (Summer)
The Twosies - Book 5 (Fall)
The Twosies – Book 6 (Winter)
The Twosies - Book 7 (Spring)
The Twosies - Book 8 (Summer)

More Josie Brown Novels
The Candidate
Secret Lives of Husbands and Wives
The Baby Planner

How to Reach Josie

To write Josie, go to:
mailfromjosie@gmail.com

To find out more about Josie, or to get on her eLetter list for book launch announcements, go to her website:
www.JosieBrown.com

You can also find her at:

www.AuthorProvocateur.com

twitter.com/JosieBrownCA

facebook.com/josiebrownauthor

pinterest.com/josiebrownca

instagram.com/josiebrownnovels